Taino

Donald H Sullivan
~~*~~

Dedication

To all the present day descendants of the Taino who once populated the islands of the Caribbean, and who now mostly reside in Hispaniola (Kiskeya) and Puerto Rico (Boriken.)

Table of Contents

Introduction

The Taino people populated the islands of the Caribbean when Columbus landed in The New World. The Taino originated in South America in regions near the Amazon and the Orinoco. They were known there as the Arawak, but became known as the Taino after migrating to the Caribbean.

The Taino shared the Caribbean islands with another people called the Carib. The Carib were a warlike people who practiced cannibalism.

When Columbus first landed in The New World, he was greeted by the friendly Taino . At the outset, things went well between the two cultures, but then Columbus claimed the land they were on as a territory of Spain. He demanded tribute from the Taino, to be paid in gold to the King and queen of Spain.

When they could not produce enough gold, Columbus punished them, and took some as slaves back to Spain. Relations soured, and there were soon clashes between the Spaniards and the Taino.

~~*~~

Part I: Kiskeya (Hispaniola)

The Beginning

In many eons past, in the area we now call the Caribbean, volcanic activity under the sea caused upheavals of unimaginable violence. At the end of a long period of volcanic violence an arc of islands began to emerge from the sea, a result of the submarine volcanic eruptions.

In the beginning the islands were hot, steaming wastelands, devoid of life. Ages passed and the islands cooled. More ages passed as the islands were overlain by soluble rock such as limestone, which was conducive to forming the many caves in the islands. After many years of erosion of the volcanic rock and limestone by wind and rain, plus layer upon layer of wind borne dust from the plains of Africa and surrounding land masses, arable soil formed on the islands.

Eons passed and vegetation began to appear, some brought by the seeds in the droppings of birds and others washed ashore by tidal and wave action. The islands were finally fit for habitation.

One of these islands was a small, irregular rectangle-shaped island, which would later be called Boriken by its inhabitants.

Meanwhile, much farther to the north, the latest ice age had caused a land bridge to form between Asia and North America. Various tribes from different parts of Asia used the bridge to cross over into then uninhabited North America, and from there on into South America. These tribes of various Asiatic races split up and formed many different cultures and nations throughout the Americas.

From them sprang cultures like the Sioux, Navajo, and Cherokee in the north, and Incas, Aztecs, and Mayans in the south. Also included were the Arawak people of the Orinoco and Amazon regions of South America. From them sprang the Taino people who populated the Caribbean.

Arawak

Migua stood in the crowd and watched as Surani was escorted to the sacrificial table. She was being led up the steps of the platform where the table rested. She was, in Migua's eyes, the most beautiful girl in all creation. Her slim, tanned body moved with the grace of a Jaguar. She held her head high as she climbed the steps.

The sacrifice would be with much ceremony. Surani would be placed on the stone table with its ornately chiseled images. The sacrificial knife, also ornately decorated, lay on a stand next to the table.

Caobara, the high priest and great boheek of the region, was now blessing the rope which would hold Surani to the table, and an assistant was preparing the cup of brew, especially prepared to keep her in a stupor during the proceedings.

But with all the rituals and formalities, Migua saw it as nothing less than the murder of the girl who was his bride to be. He had only recently reached the age of marriage, and she would reach the age in one more season.

But Surani had disobeyed the edict of their leader, Gocatai, the supreme kaseek of this region.

Migua brushed the coarse black hair away from his eyes as he watched. The muscles under his bronze skin tensed. He balled his fists and clenched his teeth.

Gocatai mounted the stairs to the platform and a hush came over the crowd. The great kaseek held his hands up, palms facing inward, and then slowly turned, facing each direction.

"My honored high priest, Caobara, was given a sign by Yakahu that our people must observe a day of fasting, to begin on the first morning and end on the second morning the following day.

"Yakahu decreed that nothing was to be taken into our bodies but water from dawn to dawn of the fast. As advised by Caobara, I issued a proclamation announcing the day of Fast." He looked down at the form of Surani, now secured to the sacrificial table.

"This virgin maiden chose to ignore me, to ignore Caobara, and to ignore Yakahu himself. The penalty for such an offense is death. She must be sacrificed to appease Yakahu."

"It's not a sacrifice at all," Migua whispered to his best friend, Kokyu, who stood beside him. "It's punishment. They just call it sacrifice because they think it justifies the killing. They gave no consideration to the fact that she had been sick and could not eat for two days just before the fast began."

"Yes," said Kokyu, "She was starving. Her crime was trying to sneak a piece of dried fish."

Migua saw the fear in Surani's eyes as the boheek was blessing the knife. They had not yet given her the brew.

"We must act before they give her the brew so that she will be clear headed," said Migua. When I give the signal we must all act in unison, each doing our part in carrying out the plan. If we fail, all eight of us will end up being sacrificed."

The boheek held the cup up and began mumbling his blessing. As he did, Migua began screaming. "The Anaki! The Anaki! To your weapons." The Anaki simply meant enemy, and it meant a tribe with which the Arawak had long been at war for decades, a war of raids, pillaging and ambushes.

10

Several well-hidden accomplices of Migua began beating Anaki-sounding drums and yelling their battle cries. Confusion ensued. Everyone was running to their house for weapons. The kaseek and the boheek both jumped from the platform and started screaming for order as they followed the crowd.

Migua and Kokyu leapt on the platform and cut the ropes, freeing Surani. He grabbed her hand. "Come on," he said. "To the river."

As they ran toward the Orinoco, they could hear the shouts of the kaseek barking orders. By now he would have realized that he had been tricked, and would be organizing an armed party for pursuit.

When Migua reached the river he found that the others had already reached the bank of the Orinoco and were waiting for him and Surani. The two dugout canoes they had chosen had already been secretly provisioned. They could have chosen one of the longer canoes, to hold twenty or more people, but it would be wiser to use two smaller, more maneuverable canoes.

The two dugouts could each hold ten people for a total of twenty, so with only nine people there would be plenty of room for provisions, plus room to take turns napping and resting.

~~*~~

They were soon in the strong river current and heading out toward the sea. Migua was confident that they had enough of a head start to reach the sea well ahead of their pursuers.

Surani was seated behind Migua. She leaned forward, put her arm around his neck, and kissed him on the cheek, then leaned back and resumed rowing. "Thank you, my Dearest, thank you. I had a deep inner feeling that you were planning something." She laughed nervously. "But I was scared when they tied me down."

"I didn't mean to scare you, but I wanted to wait for the best moment to catch them unaware." He paused. "The open sea is just ahead and there are no pursuers in sight. We have made it."

"But where are we going?" Asked Surani. "We can never go back to Orinoco country."

"To the islands of the north," he said, "We will choose one of the islands and settle there. There are a people there called the Taino who speak Arawak, our language. Traders from our village who have gone there say they are a very gentle and friendly people."

Kokyu, who was seated in front of Migua spoke up. "Yes, but the traders also speak of a people called the Carib, who are not so friendly. They attack, pillage, and kill just as our Anaki do. Only they are worse; they are cannibals who barbeque and eat their enemies."

"The Carib do not inhabit the same group of islands as the Taino," said Jujo, who was seated in front, and was considered the best navigator in their party. Jujo was a man of many seasons; his hair now showing streaks of gray. At one time he had two wives, but one had been killed in a raid by the Anaki and the other had died from a fever.

"I made a trip with the traders several times, and talked with some of the Taino. The Carib are from a group of smaller islands to the south and east of the Taino islands."

"How are we going to choose our island?" said Surani.

"I have been thinking about that," answered Migua. If all agree, I say we choose the first one we see, providing that the people there will accept us."

"There is a large island called Kiskeya," said Jujo, "where the Taino are very friendly and would welcome us. I will guide us there if you agree."

Migua looked at the others, who nodded. "Very well," said Migua. "Kiskeya it is."

They reached the mouth of the river and the little wooden canoes were now bobbing like corks. They paddled the canoes past the rough waters at the mouth of the Orinoco and were now on the open sea, heading north.

~~*~~

Migua awakened to the gentle shaking of Kokyu. He stretched and reached for a hard, flat piece of cornbread and a small portion of dried fish. He noted that the sky was brightening in the east; it was the beginning of the fifth day.

There were strong winds now and the waves were getting bigger. Migua slid overboard and swam around for a few moments in the rough water before pulling himself back aboard the canoe.

He then relieved Kokyu and took his turn rowing.

"We're almost there," said Jujo. "We should reach Kiskeya before the sun is high. But I don't like the looks of this weather. In this part of the sea they have bad storms. The Taino call them hurrikains. If we are lucky we will reach Kiskeya before it gets much worse."

But as the day wore on the weather continued to worsen. The sky was now dark and it was now impossible to tell the position of the sun. The wind was growing stronger and the waves were swelling to ever greater heights.

At one point, when their little craft was atop a huge swell, Surani tapped him on the shoulder and pointed.

13

"Migua, look!"

Migua made out a white shoreline in the distance.

"Jujo, I think we have reached Kiskeya. We have spotted land over to our left."

But as he spoke, the little canoe spun around, and what had been their left was now their right. The craft was out of control now. The other canoe was now lost from sight.

Migua looked up and saw the monstrous wave coming at them, but it was too late. He tried frantically to turn the canoe to face the wave, but his paddle might as well have been a blade of grass. Had the wave hit head on they might have had a chance. But it hit from the side and the canoe capsized.

Migua came up for air. Sputtering, he looked around, trying to spot Surani or any of the others. None were to be seen. Though the shoreline he had seen was distant, he did not deem it too far to swim, for the Arawak of the Orinoco were superb swimmers, having defeated many other tribes in water sports.

But even so, none of them had experience swimming in waters like this, for the squalls of the Orinoco were not nearly so severe. Anyway, he was now unsure of the direction in which he had seen land. He waited, hoping that a swell would lift him high enough to see the land again. But as he waited, he felt a painful bump on the right side of his head.

His vision blurred as he reached out to grab the object that had hit his head. It was the canoe. He grasped for it but only succeeded in pushing it away. He felt himself being lifted again, but when he reached the crest of the wave his vision was too blurry to search for land.

"Migua, Migua!" Amid the howling of the wind he heard his name, but only barely. He was sure it was Surani. He could not see, but he answered her call. "Surani, can you see me? I have been blinded."

"I saw you but I have lost you again. I'm searching for you."

"Can you see land?"

"Yes but I only get glimpses of it."

"Don't stay here and waste your energy. Start swimming toward shore, and keep calling. I'll try to follow the sound of your voice."

"No. I won't leave you. I will stay in place and call to you."

A moment later she called. "Over here."

He swam toward the sound, "I hear you."

After several more calls, her voice started getting farther away and then fading away in the howling wind. He was not surprised. In this rough water it would be difficult to stay in one place very long. And in the roaring wind it would be hard to fix the direction of a voice.

He strained to hear her voice again, but knew there would be little chance of it. If anything, these stormy waters would pull them farther apart.

But just as he was ready to give up hope, his eyes began to come back into focus. He was rising to the crest of another swell, and when he looked around he saw the white, sandy beach, a little nearer than before.

But he did not start swimming for shore, for he feared that Surani would still be trying to locate him and might become too exhausted to reach shore. He began looking for her each time he reached the crest of a swell. There was nothing but the churning, heaving waters everywhere he looked.

But the next time he crested his heart leaped, for he saw a lone figure crawling out of the heavy surf onto the beach. It had to be Surani. He started swimming toward shore.

When he neared the beach, he encountered strong undercurrents in the heavy surf, and was almost pulled under several times. It took him longer than expected and he was tiring when his feet finally touched bottom.

The person he had seen on the beach started running toward him. But it was not Surani, it was Kokyu. He was happy to see his good friend, but was disheartened at the thought that Surani was still struggling to find him in the stormy water.

The two clasped hands and embraced.

Migua took a deep breath and exhaled. "I've got to go back for Surani. She's still out there in the sea, and she's searching for me."

Kokyu shook his head. "No, no, you're too exhausted. If you try to go back now you'll drown. And the wind seems to be getting even stronger..."

"But I've got to go. She thinks I am still blinded and is looking for me." He explained to Kokyu about the canoe hitting his head, and how Surani was trying to guide him with her voice.

"She won't give up until she finds me."

"Migua, look at that water. Even if you were rested it would be difficult swimming. But in your condition you would surely drown. By going out there you will not be helping her, yourself, or anyone."

"But at least I must let her know that I can see now. And besides, if she is lost to the sea because of me I could never forgive myself. I must go."

Kokyu stepped back and nodded. "If you must, I won't try to stop you."

Migua turned and trotted toward the pounding surf. "Goodbye, my friend."

But as he neared the surf, he stopped short. Something was out there. A piece of driftwood? The canoe? But his heart leaped when he saw that it was neither...it was a swimmer. And then he spotted another, there were two of them.

He could barely make them out, but it could only be Surani and Jujo.

Kokyu ran up beside him. The two were silent as they watched and waited. When the swimmers approached the churning surf near the shoreline, obviously exhausted and struggling, Migua and Kokyu swam out to help them in.

When they reached shallow water, Migua found the strength to lift her, and struggling against the gusting winds, carried her to the beach. He gently put her down, and then collapsed, falling beside her. Still lying there and gasping for breath, they embraced.

"I...I was looking for you in the water and saw Jujo. I asked him to help me find you." She gasped and caught her breath again. "Then we saw you two on the beach...you can see now?"

He explained to her about regaining his sight and then seeing Kokyu on the beach and thinking it was her.

"Yakahu has been kind to us this day."

"We had better move to higher ground," said Jujo, "the wind is getting stronger and the water is rising. It's good that we reached shore before the hurrikain reached full force."

They made it to the wall of palms and thick tropical growth lining the shore, which helped to diminish the power of the wind to some extent. They moved on through the brush to higher, hilly ground. They were safe from the rising water of the sea, but now a drenching rain was pouring down.

"There are caves all over Kiskeya," said Jujo, "we should have no trouble finding one for shelter."

He had no sooner spoken than Surani announced that she had spotted one. "It's just ahead and to the left," she said, "on the slope of that hill."

They ran through the howling wind and driving rain to the cave entrance. Fortunately, the wind was at their backs, for it was so strong now it would have been difficult to run against it.

"I hope no beast is in there," said Surani.

"Do not worry," said Jujo. "There are no Jaguars or large animals on Kiskeya. The biggest animal is a crocodile, but we needn't fear them here."

They were drenched, and the dry cave was welcome.

"I noticed some brush just inside the cave entrance," said Migua. I think there are some dead twigs and fronds that are dry enough to start a fire."

He pulled off the cotton headband, and after checking it, decided that it would serve as a spinner. They set about gathering twigs and branches.

Migua accepted the task of starting the fire. Even though he was good at it, he knew it would be a painstaking job, requiring time and patience.

"I wonder if those in the other canoe made it," said Jujo.

"I hope so," said Kokyu. "I just hope they didn't get caught in a current that pulled them farther away from the

18

island. We weren't too far from shore, but even so we were lucky to make it."

Jujo nodded. "This is a terrible storm. I heard the Taino speak of these hurrikains, but I did not believe they could be this bad. If those in the other canoe did make it, they will probably be a long way from where we came ashore."

A wisp of smoke began to curl up from the twigs, and moments later a small flame appeared. Before long, Migua had a small fire going. Night was falling and the small flame gave off enough light to cheer the four of them. They agreed that they would take turns through the night, with one staying awake to tend the fire.

They gathered some of the wet shrubs and piled them near the fire to dry out.

The wind outside was now roaring and the rain was coming down in torrents, but they were far enough inside the cave to keep warm and dry.

"The fire is comfortable." Kokyu chuckled. "Look, Jujo and Surani are already asleep."

"You get some sleep, too," said Migua. "I'll keep first watch on the fire."

~~*~~

Guacanagari

Surani, the last to keep watch, awakened the others when daylight brightened the cave entrance.

They left the cave and found that it was now calm except for occasional wind gusts. The sun was out and vapor was rising from the drying ground.

"There's plenty of fruit growing wild on Kiskeya," said Jujo. "Let's look around."

"I'm hungry," said Kokyu. "I can eat a whole tree full of fruit. Maybe we can find some animals for meat..."

He never finished the sentence. The surrounding brush and trees came alive with men armed with spears. There were about ten of them.

One of the men stepped forward. "Who are you? Where do you come from?"

Migua answered, "We are from the Orinoco region, far to the south of here."

"You are traders?"

The Taino spoke Arawak with a slightly different accent but Migua had no trouble understanding him.

Migua hesitated. Jujo had told them that the Taino had similar laws as the Arawak on fasting, and it was forbidden to break the fast. He did not like lying, but the group of nine had all agreed they would claim to be traders, and had lost their wares in a squall. The hurrikain served to support that story.

"Yes. We are sorry to say that we have lost our canoes and our wares. Also, we became separated from the rest of our group."

"Come with us. We will escort you to our village. It is only a short way. Our kaseek, Guacanagari, will decide what to do with you."

~~*~~

The village was but a short walk from the cave. It was of large, round thatched huts with conical roofs, which they later learned were called bohios. Several of the huts were badly

20

damaged by the storm. The Arawaks were led through the village until they reached a square hut, the dwelling of the kaseek. After a short wait, they were told that one of them could go in. The other three chose Migua, who followed one of the escorts in.

Guacanagari sat upon a wooden seat, similar to the one used by the kaseek at Orinoco. He was fairly young for a kaseek. He wore a full-feathered headdress, shell necklaces around the neck, shell bracelets around the upper arms and lower legs, and a breechcloth.

He motioned for Migua to be seated on the floor of clean white sand. "I have been told that you are traders from the south."

"Yes, Great Chief, but we lost our wares and canoes in the storm."

"Yes, this hurrikain was a strong one. We have never before had one strong enough to damage our bohios. Have you traded with us before?"

"No this is the first time. But one of our party has been here before."

"I cannot offer you a canoe at this time, but you are welcome to stay here with us if you wish. Perhaps you can use our village as a trade base later on. We have traded with the peoples of Kuba to our west, the peoples of Boriken to our east, and the peoples of Bimini to the north."

"Thank you Great Chief. We would like to stay, and we can earn our keep."

"Right now you must be very hungry and tired. I will have one of my assistants arrange for food. As you know, some of our bohios were destroyed during the storm, and some families must stay with others until they can be rebuilt, but I will have them fit you in somewhere."

"We do not wish to cause your people further hardship. We found a cave during the storm, and it will be comfortable enough until we can build a bohio. If your people can spare a few pallets we will be grateful."

"You can help us in the rebuilding, and we will include living spaces for the four of you where you can stay after the work is finished."

~~*~~

A deputy took them to the food line, and they lined up to receive their evening meal. Most of the food was the same as the four were accustomed to, with some variations. There was turtle meat and a stew of fish and vegetables.

Migua told his companions of his talk with Guacanagari, and all were happy with the agreements.

"While you were with the chief," said Jujo, "we talked with some of his deputies and some of the people. He is said to be a great, benevolent chief, fair to all."

"I talked with some of the women," said Surani, "and I will be welcome to join them in tending vegetables and making cloth, fishnets and things, and then we can share in using those things."

"You, Jujo, and I are skilled at felling trees and making canoes," said Kokyu, "so they want our help with canoe making. I told them we're good at canoeing and fishing, too. I mentioned that we are good at archery and could be of help in hunting, but they say they use archery only in war, not hunting."

"We can do our share," said Migua, "and Guacanagari says that later on he will provide us with canoes for trading. But first we must help with the rebuilding of the damaged bohios."

They finished the meal and returned to the cave.

~~*~~

The four Arawaks were not familiar with the Taino bohios, but soon learned their methods of construction. The bohios were large enough to accommodate several families. They were mainly used for resting and sleeping quarters, as the Taino shared everything and did all activities on a communal basis.

On the fourth day they had just finished their evening meal and were preparing to return to the cave when someone shouted, "The Carib, the Carib!"

Chaos ensued. People were yelling and running in all directions. The Carib were now pouring into the village. Their bodies and faces were painted and they were carrying spears, clubs, and bows and arrows.

Several shot flaming arrows onto the roofs of the bohios, which quickly went up in flames. Migua looked around for his companions but did not find them. He picked up a pole used for construction of the bohios. It was of stout hardwood and would serve as a good club. If only he had his bow. He had been one of the best with the bow in Orinoco.

Some of the Taino had now armed themselves and were fighting back. He joined a group just in time to ward off an attack by a band of Carib who were fighting in a frenzy. His club caught one of the raiders with a hard blow to the knees. The man went down screaming in pain.

Just as suddenly as the attack had started, it was over. The Carib were retreating, but they were carrying a number of captives with them. The Carib warriors had also picked up their wounded and were carrying them away.

He noted that the Taino did not follow and attack the retreating Carib, but simply allowed them to retreat.

Most of the captives of the Carib were young women, being pulled by ropes which were looped around their bodies. Migua gasped, for he saw that one of the young women was Surani. Without thinking, he charged the warrior that was pulling her.

The surprised warrior was caught off guard, apparently not expecting a Taino attack from the rear. Migua's club caught him behind his skull, making a sharp thud. The warrior dropped like a rock. Migua grabbed the rope and Surani followed him back to the village.

Migua was surprised that the Carib had not attacked him; instead they seemed more concerned with carrying off the warrior he had felled.

~~*~~

The next day, Anagani, a deputy to Guacanagari was telling the group something they already knew. "We have reconstructed five of the Bohios, but the Carib destroyed six. This means that you will have to wait longer for a bohio." She looked at Migua and smiled. "What you did yesterday in rescuing Surani was great, but it could have consequences.

"There is an unspoken agreement that the Carib will attack to carry off as many girls as they can for their wives, in addition to any plump young men for the barbeque pit.

"We are expected to resist, but if we become too aggressive sometimes they come back in greater force for revenge. Since yours was an attack by a lone man, they will probably let it go."

"I don't want to be the cause of another attack," said Migua, "but I could not let them take my bride to be." He paused. "They were very concerned about taking their dead and wounded with them. Are they always like that?"

"They consider it a dishonor to leave their dead or wounded among the enemy. If they can't take them during a battle, they come back to reclaim them. We offer no resistance if they come in peace."

The Taino are a peaceful people, Migua thought, perhaps too peaceful. The Carib take what women they want and even take some people to feed on, like animals. The Taino never counter-attack. They reason that by giving up a few of their people they avoid all-out war with the Carib...a powerful and cruel enemy.

The Arawak of the Orinoco never let their enemies get away with raids. They will counter attack and make raids of their own. But the Arawak and the Anaki fight because of a deep hatred of each other, because of some long ago dispute. As Migua understood it, the Carib raided only to get captives, and when they got what they wanted they retreated.

He was accepted as a Taino now and must adapt to their ways. They are not cowardly; he could see that in their attitude. It also showed when they chose to fight. But something in their

24

nature rejected war. Except for their peaceful nature, the Taino were very much like the Arawak. Both had the same features and spoke the same language. Some of their customs and traditions were the same. He and his Arawak companions should find it easy to adapt.

On some afternoons the deputy chiefs would allow them to stop work and participate in sports. Migua loved their ball game called batey, and he immediately proved to be good at it. It was very similar to the game played by the Arawak.

But he excelled at water sports. The Taino were the best he had ever competed with, but he won all his contests and the Taino marveled at his skill. Surani, Kokyu, and the grizzled Jujo were also skilled at water sports, but could do no better than come out even in contests with the Taino.

~~*~~

The Bohios were finally completed. A bohio was large dwelling, so several families were assigned to each bohio. Migua's group was assigned to a dwelling with two large families. One of the men had five wives and the other had three. There were twelve children in all, but there was still plenty of room for Migua's group.

After the evening meal, the four found their new living space. They lit their allotted candle torch, made from resin of the Tabonuco tree, and gathered around the flame, sitting cross-legged on the floor. Several curious children stood nearby watching the new people.

"We have been here for over one moon and have heard nothing from those in the other canoe," said Jujo. "I don't think they made it to shore, or we would have heard from them by now."

"Maybe they were lucky enough to have not overturned," said Surani. "Maybe the wind and currents carried them to Kuba or another island."

Migua nodded. "They are all good canoeists, so that is possible. But they have never experienced anything like a hurrikain. It's hard to imagine they survived in such a storm."

25

It grew quiet for a few moments, except for the murmur of the conversations of other families. Kokyu broke the silence.

"I wonder what tasks the deputy chiefs will have for us tomorrow. I hope they will assign us to fishing groups."

"Me, too," said Jujo. "But they have many vegetable gardens, so we might end up tending vegetables."

"Guacanagari promised me that we would be assigned a canoe for trading at some later time, " said Migua. "A moon and more has passed. I hope he remembers."

They had worked hard that day and were tired. They doused their candle, spread their pallets, and soon all were asleep.

~~*~~

After breakfast, everyone went to their assigned tasks. Some were tending vegetables, some were sent out to gather fruit, some were sent fishing, crabbing or hunting turtles, some went to gather clams and oysters, some to make cloth or pottery, and various other tasks. Finally, the chief's deputy Anagani approached them.

"Guacanagari has decided that he wants you as traders. He wants you to go to Bimini. We have groups of traders going to Kuba, and Boriken, but none to Bimini yet. You will be given a large canoe so that you can take plenty of trading goods. The four of you will go, and Maiya will go with you. She has been to Bimini before.

"The trading goods are now stored in game court. Since you are experienced traders, Guacanagari is depending on you to use your trading skills to acquire some valuable items for us. Maiya will be waiting for you at the game court."

The four of them set out for the game court, where the game of batey was played. The court was nearly identical to the batey court in the Orinoco region.

"Among us, only Jujo has experience trading, so we must be careful not to mention this to Maiya. She is a close friend of Havani, one of Guacanagari's favorite cousins. If Guacanagari knew this, he might banish us...or worse."

26

Do not worry," said Jujo. "You have seen traders from other lands bargaining with our people in Orinoco. Just try to do as they did."

~~*~~

After loading the trading goods on the canoe, the five of them set out.

"I hope we don't have another storm," said Surani.

"The storm season has passed," said Maiya. "The one that you experienced was the last."

"We have never been to Bimini," said Migua, "what is it like?"

"It is not an island. It is part of a great land mass. But Bimini is surrounded by the sea on all sides except for the north, where it connects to the land mass. In the south part is a people called the Takesta that we have traded with. Their land lies between a big lake and the sea.

"They are a friendly people, but their neighbors, a people called the Calusa, are hostile toward strangers. They tell us of a people to the north, called the Timucua, who are also peaceful. It is the Takesta that we will visit on this trip."

~~*~~

They paddled through some off-shore islands and entered the mouth of a river called the Maiyami. A small crowd of Takestas was awaiting them on the river bank. They greeted the five Taino and helped them beach their canoe. One spoke halting, but understandable Arawak.

"We will go tell our kaseek you are here. We must get his permission to trade."

They left, and moments later they saw more canoes entering the mouth of the river.

"These must be some of their people returning from fishing," said Migua. "I see about eight canoes."

"They are all small," observed Surani. "Only one or two people to a canoe."

27

Maiya shaded her eyes, watching the approaching dugouts. "They do not have large trees here as we have in Kiskeya, so they can't make big canoes."

Migua surveyed the surrounding land. It was flat with shrubs, small trees, and scattered palms. "I don't see a single one large enough..."

Maiya held up her hand, signaling him to stop. "They are turning their canoes toward us, and I don't think they are Takestas."

Migua noticed spears and clubs among them. This was no fishing party, he thought.

They watched as the group landed and beached their canoes. There were twelve of them. As they approached on foot, Maiya held up her hand in a sign of friendship.

"Greetings. We are Taino from Kiskeya and we are traders."

The leader stepped forward, then motioned one of his group to come forward with him. He then muttered something to the man.

"I am interpreter for our leader. He says to tell you we are Calusa."

The leader spoke again.

"He wants to know what you have to trade," said the interpreter.

Maiya went to the canoe and uncovered the goods.

Migua did not like the way this was going. He eyed the canoes of the Calusa party and saw nothing but a few fish. The leader noticed Migua checking the dugouts..

He laughed. "We will trade you fish," he said.

"You are joking," said Maiya. "We have valuable items here."

The leader reached down into the canoe and picked up a shell necklace. He grimaced and threw it back into the canoe. He then picked up a small wooden bowl and examined it. After throwing the bowl back into the dugout, he picked up another

28

necklace, this one with gold ornaments strung on it. He smiled and said something to the interpreter.

"He says he likes this one. He will give you a fish."

Maiya frowned. "I am not simple-minded. That necklace is of gold, and the ornaments were made by one who is a master at his trade."

Migua stepped up and stood by Maiya. "You are not serious," he said. "You have nothing to trade but fish?" He held up his arm and motioned toward the sea. "The water is full of fish. If you have nothing of value to trade, please go in peace."

The leader said something and several men started taking goods out of the canoe.

"No!" Maiya tried to step between the men and the canoe.

Migua joined her, but as he did, from the corner of his eye he saw one of the Calusa coming at him with a club. He made to jump out of the way, but was not in time. The huge club caught him on the shoulder and knocked him to the ground. Kokyu rushed to help him, grabbing the club and jerking it from the man's grasp. But Migua was horrified to see a Calusa charging Kokyu with a spear. Kokyu attempted to pull back, but the spear caught him in the chest, impaling him.

The Calusa pulled the spear from the fallen Kokyu and turned toward Migua. Migua grabbed a canoe paddle as he jumped up, and swung with all his might at the man with the spear. He heard a crunching sound as the hardwood oar caught the man squarely in the face. The man dropped, blood pouring from his head.

The entire group of Calusa were now grabbing their clubs and spears.

Migua shouted at his companions, "To the water, it's our only chance!"

Even as he shouted he was diving into the river, with Jujo, Surani, and Maiya immediately following. As they swam away from shore, the few Calusa who had spears hurled them at the fleeing swimmers. Fortunately none of the Calusa were armed with bows. Migua felt a hit on his thigh, but it was only the spear shaft brushing against his leg. The spears stopped falling; the Calusa had apparently thrown all they had.

Migua glanced back. The Calusa were now scampering into their dugouts as a large crowd of Tekestas approached. The swimmers turned toward shore, taking care to avoid the canoes of the departing Calusa.

~~*~~

Kokyu did not survive the spear wound, and the Tekesta agreed to bury him in their burial mound, and also to remove his head and burn the flesh from the skull. They would keep his skull until the Taino returned to get it--and his spirit--and take it back to Kiskeya to be among friends.

The Calusa that Migua clubbed in the face also did not survive, and the Tekesta promised to leave his corpse in the wilderness for the vultures to feed on.

Migua learned from the Tekestas that the party of Calusa was probably a renegade band. The Tekesta had good relations with the Calusa, and though the Calusa were hostile with many, they seldom bothered the peaceful Tekesta. But sometimes renegade bands were a problem. When the Calusa organized war parties, they were much larger than the band they had encountered.

After the burial of Kokyu, and Migua said goodbye to his friend, he and his group brought out and displayed their wares. The Tekesta brought tanned skins, wooden figurines, colorful feathers, shell ornaments, and various other items.

Migua was happy to see that his first experience as a trader went so well. The Tekestas seemed happy with the trade, and everyone in his group was happy. He was sure that Guacanagari would approve of the trade, and would keep some of the items and distribute some among the people.

~~*~~

Guacanagari was happy as were his people. The skins were popular, since there were no fur bearing animals on Kiskeya. The kaseek chose a large pelt with soft, fine fur and decided he

30

would have it made into a short cloak to cover his shoulders. Maiya set two of the skins aside.

She giggled. "These will be for me and Havani. We are both not yet married, but we can make aprons of these to cover our groins after we are married."

Surani laughed. "Do either of you have a prospect for marriage yet?"

"Gohuana has spoken for me, but he already has too many wives. Several suitors have spoken for Havani, but she is not interested yet. She is Guacanagari's cousin, so she can be choosy."

"That is so," said Surani. "But she cannot choose my Migua. He has already spoken for me and I have consented. He has also said that he wishes no other wife but me." She smiled. " He and I have talked it over. I am now of age, and we have asked the kaseek to marry us and he has agreed. There will be no formal ceremony, only vows before the kaseek."

~~*~~

Three days later, Guacanagari performed the marriage in a simple ceremony, after which they were excused from daily activities for two days. During the vows, Surani donned her apron, to indicate that she was no longer available.

"By donning your apron," the kaseek intoned, "you acknowledge that you are no longer available to others."

"I so acknowledge," she responded.

She looked up at Migua and smiled. "I have never been available to others, and it will always be so."

They embraced, and their lips met in a tender but passionate kiss.

~~*~~

Migua's group made regular trading trips to Kuba and other islands with much success. They also returned to Bimini, where they recovered the skull of Kokyu from the Tekesta. Migua placed the skull on a high storage shelf in the bohio so that his friend's spirit would be near him.

In between trading trips, Migua and Jujo joined the fishing groups, while Surani and Maiya helped with cooking, making cloth, or making pottery.

On the tenth day after their return from their last trip to Bimini, Anagani called them together.

"Guacanagari wants you to return to Bimini," she said, "but this time he wants you to go farther up the coast to the territory of the Timucua people. There have been very few trading expeditions there in the past, but they have better goods to trade than the Tekesta. The Timucua are peaceful, but unlike the Tekesta, they are powerful. The Calusa do not bother them."

They proceeded to the pick-up point where the trading goods and provisions awaited them. They would be taking a longer canoe this time, for they would be carrying a bigger load of trading goods, and since this was a long journey, they needed to take more provisions.

"This will be a long trip, but we will not need to worry about the renegade bands this time," said Jujo. "I have never visited the Timucua, but I have heard much about them. Like the Tekesta, there are a few Arawak speakers among them. In times past, some Arawaks must have left their place of birth, just as we did, and went to Bimini."

"Or maybe some Taino left Kiskeya to go there in times past," said Maiya.

They arrived at the pick-up point and were sorting and inspecting the goods when several people ran past them, running toward the river. Then several more, followed by even more. Migua stopped one of them.

"What is happening? Where is everybody going?"

"Haven't you heard? Some strange men in three strange looking giant canoes have arrived off the coast. Everyone wants to go out in canoes to see them and greet them."

"You three wait here," said Migua, "I'd better go check our canoe."

"I want to go too, "said Surani.

She fell in behind him as he jogged toward the river, moments later joined by Jujo and Maiya.

They arrived at the river to find the long canoes gone, and only three small canoes were left. The river was dotted with canoes heading out to sea.

"We don't have a canoe that we can use for our journey," said Migua, "we'd might as well take one of the small ones and join the others to find what this is all about."

~~*~~

Columbus

It was an awesome sight. The three canoes were huge, rising to a great height above the water, with great squares of cloth rising above the canoes making them even higher. Canoes were all about, and many even swam out to see the strange scene.

"Look," said Maiya, "there are some men, standing on the side of the canoe. They are waving their hands at us. They are friendly."

"They are wearing cloth that covers their entire body," said Jujo, "and some are wearing some kind of metal on their heads and over their chests. And look, they allow the hair on their faces to grow."

Fascinated, they watched as the men on the ships lowered themselves into smaller boats and began rowing ashore. Migua and his group followed, as well as the Tainos in all the other canoes.

The strange men reached shore, and one of them, speaking in a strange tongue, stuck a stick with a piece of cloth on it in the sand. Then all the men landed their canoes and came ashore.

What happened next was unexpected. The men began approaching the Taino, who were by now gathered around them, and offering them gifts. The items they offered were truly wondrous. The Taino were wide-eyed as they received the gifts from these curious bearded men.

One of the men approached Migua. He smiled warmly as he handed him some brightly colored ornaments. He pointed to himself. "Luis."

Migua got the idea. He pointed to himself. "Migua."

Luis began to point at objects and look at Migua quizzically. Again, Migua got the idea and began naming the objects. Migua was amazed at how well Luis was retaining the words. When Maiya walked up, Luis started to question her. Migua immediately noticed a mutual attraction between Luis and Maiya.

Suddenly there was a commotion and Migua turned to see Guacanagari himself approaching the beach. He was being carried on a sedan chair. He arose and stood up and one of the men, apparently the leader, strode over to greet him.

Anagani appeared by Migua's side and notified him that the trip to Bimini was canceled, but instructed him to get his group and retrieve the trading goods and bring them to the beach as gifts for these visitors from a strange land.

~~*~~

As the days, then weeks went by, Luis grew more and more familiar with the Arawak language. He began to interpret for the Captain General and Guacanagari.

The big canoes, Migua learned from Luis, were not canoes at all, but were called ships and served a different purpose than canoes. And the strange men called themselves Spaniards. The leader of the Spaniards was called Captain General Cristobol Colon, but for the Taino tongue, Migua found that "Quolon" was easier to pronounce and acceptable to the Spaniards.

As Migua helped Luis learn the Arawak language, Migua himself began to learn that he, too, had a facility with languages and was picking up on Spanish.

Luis made a point of visiting with Migua and his group at every opportunity, and he and Maiya made no secret of their attraction to each other. After several visits, Luis brought his young friend, Pablo, with him. On this day Maiya had brought along her friend, Havani, cousin of Guacanagari.

Pablo, like Luis, was interested in learning Arawak, and had many questions. Migua chuckled inwardly that the young Spaniard directed most of his questions toward Havani, who seemed more than happy to help him. At the end of the day, Luis and Pablo returned to their ship.

At the evening meal, Maiya teased Havani. "Ha. A certain young friend of mine has been teasing me about having a suitor from among the Spaniards, but now this young friend is flirting with a Spaniard herself."

Havani giggled and blushed. "Pablo is handsome, and he is very nice. All the other Spaniards seem rough and lustful, but he is kind and gentle." She hastened to add, "Luis is nice, too, but most of the others seem disrespectful to us."

"You are right," said Migua. "Luis and Pablo show us respect, and their leader, the Captain-General, shows Guacanagari respect. Aside from those three, I don't like the way most of the others treat us."

"They were nice at first," said Surani. "They were friendly and gave us beautiful trinkets. But as the days passed their behavior changed. When they get drunk they are worse."

They finished the evening meal and returned to their bohio.

~~*~~

The following morning Guacanagari's deputy chiefs called their various groups together. Anagani called her group together, but did not give out work assignments as was the custom. Instead she announced that one of the Spaniard's ships, that they called Santa Maria, had run aground and sank. There was no way the ship could be saved, but Quolon had asked Guacanagari for help in moving all the cargo from the ship, dismantling the ship, and bringing the lumber ashore.

"Our kaseek has granted Quolon permission to use the ship's timber to build a small fortress on our land. They will call their fortress La Navidad. It is a wise decision by Guacanagari,

35

for he believes that La Navidad will discourage the Carib from raiding us."

~~*~~

Migua was outraged. "Since your Captain General left to return to his homeland, the thirty-nine men left behind at your La Navidad have gone out of control. They demand that we give them gold in tribute, and if we do not they punish us with lashings or captivity. Of all those the Captain-General left behind, only the two of you, my good friends Luis and Pablo, are showing respect for the Taino."

"I wish we could do something to help," said Luis, "but the man appointed as commander of La Navidad is Diego de Arana, and he is a greedy and spiteful man. He encourages the men to demand gold and to mistreat the Taino. Pablo and I have been thinking of petitioning the commander for better treatment of your people. So far we have two others who are with us."

Jujo smiled. "That is kind of you. But many of us think that Guacanagari has been too patient with the Spaniards. He reasons that the Spaniards will help him fight the Carib, but the Spaniards are becoming worse than the Carib."

"Yes," agreed Migua, "and there is talk of an uprising if the Spaniards continue to treat us as if they are our superiors. Our kaseek does not want an uprising among us, but if enough of us participated, even he would have no choice but to approve."

Pablo nodded. "I would not blame your people if they did rise up against us. I think Guacanagari opposes an uprising because he promised the Captain-General that he would allow him to build La Navidad on his land, and therefore he feels responsible for the security of the men in the fortress. He very much respects the Captain-General, and does not want to break his promise."

"Perhaps that is so," Migua, agreed, "but I think he also fears Quolon. It is said that Quolon plans to return with a much larger force, and Guacanagari does not wish to do anything to anger him."

~~*~~

Luis and Pablo strolled along the shore, watching the waves rolling in from the open sea and crashing on the white, sandy beach with a constant roar. Pablo Menendez, formerly the cabin boy of the Santa Maria, was now out of his teens and the armorer's helper at La Navidad. Luis de Torres, a linguist who had a talent for learning languages and spoke several, was the interpreter for the settlement. Luis had many friends among the Taino people, who greatly respected him. Pablo and Luis strolled without speaking for a long while.

Luis spotted something half buried in the sand. He stooped and picked up the object. "A lantern from the Santa Maria," he muttered. "This is near the spot where she ran aground."

"A tragic end for a good ship," said Pablo. "But we were lucky that it was in shallow water and we were able to salvage the cargo and timbers. If the helmsman hadn't been groggy from drink, the tragedy wouldn't have happened. The Santa Maria would now be with the Pinta and the Nina on the return voyage to Spain."

"And we would be aboard," said Luis, "instead of waiting here for the return of the Captain-general."

Pablo noted that the sun was almost directly overhead. "We'd better get back to La Navidad. It's almost time for the meeting. I wonder what Diego wants to tell us."

~~*~~

Diego de Arana, commander of La Navidad, stood facing the thirty-eight men making up the settlement. "I have called this meeting because I have it that some of you are unhappy with the way I run this fortress and are attempting to stir up trouble." He looked directly at Pablo. "Mutiny is punishable by death. But I am a fair man, and am willing to hear you out if you have a complaint. Does anyone wish to speak?"

Pablo stood up. "We do not seek to incite a mutiny, but we object to the way we are treating the Taino. The Taino are expected to find gold for us, and if they do not, we punish them. Some have died from beatings. Some of our men get drunk and terrorize the village. There have been cases of rape."

"We must do whatever is necessary to find gold," Diego countered. "The Captain-general himself ordered us to seek gold during his absence. That is why we are here."

"Yes, but he also ordered us to treat the Taino with respect. He became good friends with Guacanagari. He will not be happy with the way we have been conducting ourselves."

Diego was annoyed. "He will not be unhappy if we have gold awaiting him on his return."

"I think we will find little gold on the island of Hispaniola. The Taino have told us that most of their gold trinkets were acquired by trading with people from other lands."

"They lie. They do not want to reveal the location of their mines. But we will find them eventually."

"Maybe. But here is something you should know. Luis and I have learned that some among the Taino are growing restless. There is talk of an uprising by renegades, and even Guacanagari may not be able to stop it."

Diego snorted. "You expect me to believe that? The Taino are cowards. We are well-armed and well-trained fighters. They would not dare attack us."

"We are but thirty-nine," Pablo said. "Guacanagari's people number in the thousands. They are a gentle people, but if they become outraged enough to attack, we would have no chance."

"Pablo Menendez, I hear that you have become entangled with a Taino whore..."

"Havani is no whore! She is a cousin of Guacanagari. He would not be pleased to hear her called a whore."

"Do you think I care if he is displeased?" Diego raised his voice. "I want all of you to hear this. Starting now, there will be no more relationships with these women." He smiled. "By that, I don't mean I forbid a little romp in the grass now and then." There were chuckles, hoots, and scattered applause among the men.

Diego continued. "We are normal, healthy men. These Taino women run around naked, and they are attractive. But I

38

repeat--do not get involved in an intimate relationship. Is that understood?"

Pablo was stunned. "But I don't understand your objection. What is the harm? Even if some of us chose to marry, what harm is done? I don't believe the captain-general would object."

"I have had enough of your insolence. It is you who have instigated unrest. You are under arrest and charged with mutiny."

Pablo was placed under guard and escorted to a small hut normally used for locking up unruly drunks. At least they hadn't put him in irons--yet. The guard, Rodrigo Perez, secured the lock and seated himself just outside the door. Pablo tried to strike up a conversation with the normally friendly, easygoing man.

"Rodrigo, what do you think of Diego's new policy?"

"Be quiet. I'm not allowed to talk with you."

"Suppose you met a Taino girl you really liked. I've never met a girl like Havani..."

"Shut up. You want to get me in trouble?"

Rodrigo was right. He was under orders not to talk. Pablo sat down on the floor and began to think about the gravity of his situation. Diego would probably arrange a speedy trial and execution to set an example. Pablo would die here, never to see Spain again.

And there was Havani. Now, more than ever, he realized how much he loved her. He had to do something; he couldn't just sit here and wait to die.

~~*~~

Havani was shocked. "I can't believe it. They have locked him up?" Her voice broke and she sobbed. "Why...how can they do that?"

"Diego de Arana is furious with him because he questioned his leadership and how he deals with your people. He had me arrested, too, but made me promise that I would behave myself if he let me go. I think that he does not lock me up because it might anger the Captain General, because I interpret for him."

"What will they do with Pablo?" Asked Maiya.

"I am afraid the commander will have him put to death, to make an example of him."

Havani gasped. "No...no...they would not do that."

"I plan to help him escape, but I will need your help."

"Just tell us what you need," said Migua.

At that point, Jujo, who had been out among those who planned to rise against the Spaniards, entered. Migua briefed him on the imprisonment of Pablo, and that they were now planning to help him escape.

"Then in that case, I can trust you with the news I have, Luis. A large group will attack La Navidad tomorrow before dawn. They know that the Spaniards only post one sentry, and he always falls asleep in the early morning."

"We had better start making plans right away," said Migua. "It will be dark soon."

~~*~~

Pablo inspected the hut. It was without windows and devoid of furnishings. The walls and roof were of stout bamboo poles lashed together. They had taken his knife, and he could find no weakness in the walls. The floor, however, consisted of sandy soil covered with palm fronds. He should have no trouble digging his way out. He sat down to await the cover of darkness.

When darkness fell, he began digging with his hands. The soil was soft, and he made good progress. He emerged on the outside of the rear wall, and as he pulled himself out, he felt a hand on his shoulder.

"Pablo, it's me," Luis whispered. "Rodrigo is asleep. Let's get out of here before he wakes up. Follow me."

Luis ran toward the beach with Pablo on his heels. When they were out of earshot of the settlement, Luis slowed to a walk.

40

"I was coming to help you escape," said Luis, "but when I arrived I saw that you were already coming out. Thank God I reached you before you ran from the guard shack or it could have ruined our plans."

"What of the other two? Did they come with you?"

"Pedro and Manuel? Those vermin! It was they who told Diego of our plans. Diego granted me amnesty on the condition that I behave myself, then released me. Later, I managed to sneak out and meet with Havani and Maiya and their group. Lucky that I did, too. I learned from them that the renegade Tainos plan to attack La Navidad tomorrow morning, just before dawn."

"My God. We tried to warn the fools, but they wouldn't listen. But what about us? Are we in danger?"

"The renegades might kill every Spaniard they see. We'd better hide until things calm down."

"What about Havani and Maiya?"

"They are in no danger. I promised Havani that I would help you escape. Maiya worried that I would be caught, but she knew that it had to be done. They know of a place where we can hide."

"That will be almost impossible," Pablo observed. "The Taino know every rock on this island."

"The girls thought of that. They arranged for a canoe with a cache of provisions to be hidden on the beach. They told me where it is hidden, and suggested we row out to a small, deserted offshore island called Nahia. The island can be seen from the point where the canoe is hidden."

"How long do they expect us to stay there?"

"When things calm down, they will send word to us. They'll send a lone messenger so we'll know it's not a war party."

The two men walked along the beach until they spotted the canoe. It was a clear, moonlit night, and they could see Nahia from where they stood.

41

They pushed the canoe into the surf and set out for the island. After reaching the island, the exhausted men stretched out on the beach and slept.

~~*~~

On the morning of the third day, they finished the last of their provisions.

"Three days and still no messenger," said Pablo. "Surely things have calmed down by now."

"The renegades may have discovered that two Spaniards are missing and are looking for us. Don't be impatient."

"It occurs to me that Guacanagari may not be too anxious to have us back on Hispaniola," said Pablo. "He knew of the attack, but did not stop them. He may be plotting to have us murdered."

"Not likely. He didn't interfere with the attack for fear that he himself might be murdered. He is a man who opposes violence. Let's wait at least one more day. I saw a couple of fruit trees; we won't starve."

"Even if Guacanagari opposes violence and would cause us no harm, there is still something else to consider. When the Captain-general returns, he'll probably suspect us as deserters and have us arrested. I have a plan to bargain with Guacanagari to hide us."

"I never thought of it that way. What is your plan?"

"We can offer to teach the Taino many things. They fear the Carib, who frequently attack and plunder their villages." I can show them how to make crossbows, catapults, and other weapons to fight the Carib. In return, they can keep our existence secret from the Captain-general."

"But how can we approach Guacanagari? The renegade Tainos may kill us before we can reach him."

"That is a chance we'll have to take," said Pablo.

They left the small island of Nahia and set course for Hispaniola. They landed, beached the canoe, and managed to drag it into nearby brush, so that it was well hidden.

We must remember to tell Maiya and Havani where the canoe is hidden so they can be retrieved. Canoes are valuable items among the Taino.

They then set out for the kaseek's village. As they approached the village, they suddenly found themselves surrounded by renegades.

Most of the renegades were armed with wooden spears, but some carried Spanish swords: evidence that the Spanish settlement had indeed been wiped out. There was nowhere to run; they were encircled. The Taino began kicking and pummeling them. Pablo went down, and one of the renegades stood over him, holding a sword to his throat.

He heard Luis shouting, apparently trying to reason with the attackers. One of the Taino stepped forward and said something to the man standing over Pablo. The man raised his sword and stepped back.

"Thank God," said Luis. "One of them recognized me."

~~*~~

Guacanagari listened intently to Pablo's proposal. "There is much you can teach us," said the chief, "but I cannot accept your offer. The Taino disdain violence. In spite of being surrounded by savage tribes like the Carib, we have survived. The recent violence shown by some of my people has sickened me, even though they were provoked by the misdeeds of your people.

"But now I fear the vengeance of my friend, Quolon. He will be outraged when he returns to find his fortress destroyed."

"I suggest you tell him that the Carib attacked the settlement," said Pablo. "He will have no reason to disbelieve you. He knows the Carib are cannibals and savages."

"Your suggestion has merit. I will give it some thought. As for you two, I have decided what to do with you."

"He's going to execute us," Pablo whispered to Luis.

The chief continued. "My cousin Havani has made a suggestion that has my wholehearted approval. As you have said, you do not wish your chief to learn of your survival." He

43

smiled, a rarity for the Great Chief. "Nor do I. I would rather you were not on this island when your chief returns.

"Havani proposes that we send you to the great land to the northwest. Havani and Maiya have agreed to go with you."

Pablo and Luis were amazed. Neither they nor any of the other Spaniards had been told of any large land mass in the vicinity called Bimini. Could this be Asia, they wondered, the land that the Captain-general had been seeking?

"But how can we get there?" Asked Pablo. "We have no ship."

"It is near enough to travel by canoe," the chief told them. "Our traders have traded with the people there."

~~*~~

Three large dugouts were outfitted for the trip. Traders who had gone there before would be their guides. Maiya had been to Bimini several times, but she had never visited the northern territory of the Timucuans.

Migua, Surani, and Jujo would not make the journey. Guacanagari considered them as his best traders, and besides, now that Luis was no longer available as interpreter, the kaseek thought that Migua had learned enough Spanish to interpret for him and Quolon.

Havani was excited about the trip and saw it as a great adventure. Pablo was amused as she talked excitedly of the coming journey.

"The traders say we will stop at several islands on the way. We will see other tribes, but they all speak Arawak, our language. Only a few of the Timucuans in the great land of Bimini speak Arawak, but the tribes there use sign language known by all.

"The people there wear coverings over their bodies, but not as much as the Spaniards do." She giggled. "But Maiya and I don't mind. Some of the coverings are very pretty."

"You will be pretty enough with or without the coverings," said Pablo.

44

She laughed, playfully kicking sand at him. "Do you know what the traders say? They say that there is a fountain up there that keeps people young. If you drink from it you will never grow old."

"A fountain of youth," said Pablo. "Let's hope the Spaniards never hear of it."

~~*~~

Quolon returned to the New World on his second voyage and learned that his settlement, La Navidad, had been destroyed and all thirty-nine men killed by Caonabo, a kaseek of the Carib. Migua interpreted for Guacanagari as he told of the attack by the Carib.

Migua never suspected that his kaseek was a cunning man, but he saw the cunning in what the kaseek was doing. Caonabo had long been a rival of Guacanagari, with Caonabo usually holding the upper hand. Unlike Guacanagari, Caonabo was a fierce leader, and it was even said that he was not really a Taino, but was born a Carib.

Guacanagari played on that, accusing the "Carib" kaseek of attacking La Navidad.

Quolon was saddened, but also angry. "I will make Caonabo pay for this," he proclaimed.

Migua could see the relief in Guacanagari's face when he was sure that Quolon believed him. He could now be sure the Spaniards would not attack his people, but instead would turn against his rival kaseek, Caonabo.

This time Quolon had brought a thousand men with him, a force that could deal with any Taino uprising. After Quolon left, Guacanagari made it plain that he would not join any uprising against the Spaniards if hostilities developed. Migua knew that the Spaniards now had a powerful force, but he was disappointed with his kaseek's attitude, even though he knew the kaseek to be a man of peace.

Migua did not trust the Spaniards. He had a fair knowledge of their language now, and overheard soldiers speaking ill of the

Taino. The Taino were ignorant, the Spaniards said, and they were cowardly.

The Spaniards planned to take all the gold they could find, make slaves of the Taino, and take the women for their own delight.

Whenever he tried to tell Guacanagari of these things, it fell on deaf ears. Apparently the kaseek had made up his mind that he would do nothing to antagonize the Spaniards.

~~*~~

Even when Quolon started demanding gold as tribute to his King and Queen in Spain, the kaseek did not protest. The Spaniards had now become their masters. Each Taino was required to bring the Spaniards a certain quantity of gold, and those who did not meet the quota had both hands chopped off.

The Spaniards love of gold was insatiable. They forced the Taino to work the mines, as well as to raise food for them. Many of the Taino were dying from starvation, forced labor, and horrible diseases carried by the Spaniards. But still the kaseek did nothing.

A few of the Spaniards were like Luis and Pablo, and sympathized with the Taino. Their shaman priest that they called de La Casas, protested the Spaniard's treatment of the Taino, but the Spanish greed for gold prevailed. Quolon himself, who at first befriended Guacanagari and his people, had succumbed to the Spanish lust for gold.

~~*~~

Because of Migua's command of the Spanish language, the kaseek had raised his status and kept him as an advisor, since Migua had learned much of the customs and ways of the Spaniards. He was not on the same level as the cacique's deputies, but he was called to participate in meetings and contribute his opinions.

Guacanagari sat on his dujo, or throne, and faced his deputies and advisors.

"I have received word of other chiefdoms being invaded by the Spaniards. Not only on territories of other kaseeks on

46

Kiskeya, but on our neighboring islands as well. I have also received word that many of the other kaseeks are planning to join together to attack the Spaniards and drive them out.

"This is folly. The Spaniards are too powerful. I have been asked to join their alliance, and I have refused."

Migua was appalled that the kaseek refused to join the alliance. He was undecided on what course of action he should take now. He and many others in Guacanagari's chiefdom disagreed with their kaseek. But Guacanagari had made up his mind. He decided that the Spaniards were much more powerful than any force the Taino, or even the fierce Carib could muster. The kaseek was so convinced of Spanish invincibility that even in the face of Spanish cruelty against his people he did not budge. To Guacanagari, the friendship of Quolon was of utmost importance.

Yet, the kaseek was still powerful, and had the power to sentence his subjects to death if they opposed him. Migua was certain that Guacanagari so feared the Spaniards that he would not tolerate any action that might antagonize them. He would not even stop at sentencing his own subjects to death, even an advisor.

And so he decided that the wisest course of action, at least for now, was to remain silent. He would be no good to anyone if he were dead, and besides he did not want to make his young wife a grieving widow.

~~*~~

The Spanish were everywhere now. More ships arrived bringing more Spaniards. Their cruelty increased. They were bringing death and disease everywhere they went. The happiness and peace that the Taino once knew were gone forever.

But as the Spanish became more and more powerful, the Taino became more and more resentful. More chiefdoms joined the resistance of the Taino, and now there was a very large force to face the Spanish. A kaseek named Caonabo was the strongest of those who opposed the Spanish.

47

Again, Guacanagari was invited to join forces with Caonabo and other kaseeks. Again, Guacanagari refused. But his own people were growing restless now.

~~*~~

Quolon was true to his word. The Spanish invaded Caonabo's territory, and although a number of the Spaniards were killed, they drove Caonabo out, and he was now hiding in the mountains. Many of Caonabo's people were killed, and some were captured and made slaves.

Migua had no love for Caonabo's people, but he could not accept the Spaniard's way of dealing with an enemy. Even the Carib, as fierce as they were, would capture only a small number of their enemy, and the number of dead on both sides was relatively small. But the Spaniard's did not stop the slaughter or taking of prisoners after the enemy was subdued.

~~*~~

The young kaseek was perplexed. "The Spaniards are continuing to pursue and slaughter all the tribes who had united against them. They appear to be worse than the warriors of Caonabo, and even worse than the Carib. And in violation of my pact with Quolon, they are now capturing and enslaving those that have cooperated with them."

"Quolon is away most of the time now," said Migua. "Those who he leaves in charge know nothing or care nothing about your friendship with Quolon. The Spaniards are interested in only three things, gold, slaves, and converting us to their Christian religion. When Quolon could find no more gold, he turned to capturing slaves. Many of them are being taken to Quolon's homeland to be sold."

Finally, the kaseek began to turn against the Spaniards. "Quolon cares nothing about the pact he made with me. I trusted him and his people. We helped him when his ship was wrecked. We gave them food from our gardens and storage houses. We allowed him to build his fortress on our land. And now he turns his back on us while his people mistreat us."

48

"From the beginning, he has looked upon us as an inferior people," said Migua. "I have even heard that he told his queen that we are a gentle people who would make good servants. He has turned a blind eye to the cruelty of his people. They chop off the hands of those who do not bring them gold. They get drunk and rape our women."

"That is how they repay us for our kindness and generosity," said Guacanagari. "I will no longer honor any agreements I made with him."

~~*~~

Migua would have been glad to see his kaseek turn against the Spaniards, but he knew that it was too late. The uprising against the Spaniards by the allied tribes had failed. If Guacanagari had joined them, it might have made a difference, but now it would never be known. Also, many of the kaseek's people were deserting.

"My people are running to the hills and mountains. There is no reason for me to stay here now. I have no territory. I control nothing. I cannot seek help from the other kaseeks, for they, too, have lost all to the Spaniards." He turned to Anagani. "Prepare a canoe for travel to Orinoco, the great land to the south. I will leave tomorrow at dawn. It is said that the people there are much like us. Perhaps the kaseek there will give me refuge."

Anaganl dispatched several of her crew who were still remaining to prepare a canoe for travel. But a short time later they returned.

"Most of the canoes are all already gone," they told her, "and the few remaining are filled with people ready to leave. They, too are going south to Orinoco, and refuse to give up a single canoe."

"But as kaseek, the canoes belong to me. I will go personally order them to provide me with a canoe."

"But Great Chief, they were already leaving, and will be gone by now," said one of the crew.

Migua wondered how the young kaseek felt now. He was born into the ruling class. He had always been in control, and the people had always obeyed his orders and catered to his wishes. Now here he was with nothing, and being ignored by his own people.

"I have no choice," said the kaseek. "I must get my wives and family together and flee to the mountains with the others. It would be foolish to stay here put myself at the mercy of the Spaniards."

Migua felt sorry for him. Except for his unwise trust of Quolon and his fear of the Spaniards, he had been a good kaseek.. His people had respected and admired him. But he had led a fairly soft life, and life in the mountains would be hard. His deputies would help him; all of them were loyal. But although they had experienced a harder life than Guacanagari, the deputies were still less prepared for life in the mountains than the average Taino.

Migua did not worry about himself and Surani. They had experienced even rougher times than most, so they would endure life in the mountains. And his friend Jujo, though graying, could take care of himself.

He left the meeting and hurried back to the bohio.

~~*~~

The village was almost empty now, and the few families that were left were getting ready to leave. It felt strange and eerie to him. There was no activity anywhere, and no children laughing and playing in the square. H arrived at the Bohio and found it empty except for Surani.

"One of the families here left for a place they knew in the mountains," she explained. "The other family wanted to go to Bimini, and asked Jujo to guide them. He agreed, and left with them. He said to tell you farewell, and hopes that you will decide to go there to meet him."

"It was wise of him to leave for Bimini," he said. "There are no Spaniards there. The mountains will be a good place to hide, but the people hiding there will always be on the run and always be on the lookout for the Spaniards. It will be a hard life."

"So you think it best that we go to Bimini?"

"I wish we could, but there are no more canoes. All of them have been taken. Even Guacanagari could not find one and is taking his family to the mountains."

She smiled. "We do have a canoe. Do you remember the canoe that Luis and Pablo used to go to the little island of Nahia? When they returned, they hid it. I overheard Luis telling Maiya where it is hidden. My Darling, we can go to Bimini.

He smiled broadly and hugged her. "Let's not delay. Let's gather our things and be on our way."

They found the canoe and stowed the woven basket holding their belongings, provisions, and the skull of Kokyu. They were soon on their way to Bimini and a new life.

~~*~~

Migua and Surani lived peacefully in Bimini, or what is now Florida. They were unaware when, in 1513, Juan Ponce de Leon, Governor of Cuba, went ashore near what is now St. Augustine, in search of the fabled Fountain of Youth.

Their children however, were there in 1565 when the Spanish established the city of St. Augustine and began to colonize Florida.

Part II: Boriken
(Puerto Rico)

Anoki

Anoki was still a boy, but was approaching manhood. He was still in the stages of learning all the things a Taino boy must know: making canoes, felling trees, making fire, constructing Taino living quarters (bohios,) making fish hooks, fishing, hunting the small game of the island, among many other things that he would learn before becoming an adult.

A part of his learning included the game of batey, a game using a ball made from the sap of rubber trees. The game could be for fun or for ceremonial events, and sometimes to settle arguments between kaseek territories, or chiefdoms.

Anoki had been looking forward to today. As a part of his training, this was the day that he and the other children, both boys and girls, would hear the stories of their people from the elder storytellers. He finished his breakfast and hurried to the batey field. He was happy to learn that the storyteller would be Uncle Chaska, an old man much loved by all.

Not only were there many children of all ages, some his age and some younger children in attendance, but there were some adults as well. Uncle Chaska seated himself on one of the stones surrounding the batey field and the children formed a half-circle facing him and seated themselves on the ground.

The old man smiled broadly, showing many missing teeth. "Welcome to all of you," he began, "and I am happy that so many have come to hear about our people." In spite of his age and his missing teeth, he spoke clearly and in a strong voice.

"Our people once lived in a great land to the south in a place we called Orinoco. There were jungles and great rivers there, filled with many creatures, such creatures as we would never dream of here in Boriken. In the jungles there are large, fierce animals called jaguars that are bigger than a man. There are snakes longer than our canoes that kill by crushing their prey, and other snakes that are poisonous and can kill a man with one bite. Yes, it was very dangerous there, and risky for anyone who dared to venture out alone."

Anoki listened intently, as Uncle Chaska told of how the Arawaks lived, and how they hunted large animals with arrows and spears.

I wish I could have been there then. It would be fun and exciting to hunt the big animals for meat and to kill the dangerous animals with my spear. There are none here. With the exception of what we get from the sea, there is nothing here but small creatures like birds, lizards, frogs and sometimes turtles.

He listened as Uncle Chaska told of Arawak culture, and of how the Taino differed in some ways from them, but still kept much of their culture as well as the language. His interest perked up again as the old man began telling of the Arawak migrating to the north.

"In those days our people were spread out over a large area, much larger than all of Boriken. Some of the kaseeks became enemies with each other and there were raids and battles. Some of the people grew tired of the endless bickering and fighting and sought to move to a more peaceful place. Arawak traders, during their travels and searches for new trading partners, brought back word of uninhabited islands to the north."

Anoki was enthralled as he listened to how some of the people left Orinoco and set out for the islands to the north. Their journey was not without danger, he learned. They sometimes encountered terrible storms, and some who were poor navigators got lost and perished. But most made it and settled on the islands, including his island of Boriken.

The old man continued, "But the ancestors of the Carib people lived in the Orinoco region, too, and some of them later followed us. But luckily they chose the islands to the south and east of us. They prefer the smaller islands, and avoid settling on the bigger ones. They raid our villages, but not constantly as they did in Orinoco. Most of the time they leave us alone." He paused. "And that is because they are busy raiding other chiefdoms. They love war, and believe that is the way to prove their manhood. They sometimes even fight each other."

During his life, Anoki could remember only a few raids.

The raids all happened so fast. I remember some being killed during the raids. My mother told me that just after I was born, my father had died from a wound. But I remember one raid where nobody was killed or even hurt. They just took some of the women and ran off. Our elders, and even our Kaseek, Guaraca, tell us it would be unwise to counter their attacks. If we get revenge, then they will come back for revenge and it will soon get like it was in Orinoco.

Uncle Chaska was finishing his story. "We must remember," he said, "that although we are descended from the Arawaks, we are now Taino. We have developed our own culture here and we have our own land."

He smiled broadly again. "I am permitted to tell you that you may have the rest of the day as play time, so go and have fun."

As Anoki was leaving, Aiyana appeared beside him. She was one of the girls of a family that lived in the same bohio as he and his family. She had been born just a few moons after Anoki, so they had grown up together. "Did you like the story of Uncle Chaska today?"

"Yes," he answered, "I liked the story. I love to learn about our people."

"I do too, and it was nice to learn something different today, besides things like preparing and cooking the food, gardening, and making cloth."

He laughed. "Yes, today was more fun than the other things we must learn. I really liked what Uncle Chaska told us about the traders. If the traders had not found the islands here, we might still be in Orinoco with the fierce animals and the giant snakes."

"Ohh! I would be afraid."

"Don't worry, I would protect you." He laughed. "But I don't believe you would really be afraid. Everybody knows that you are the best girl in the village at games, and even better than some of the boys. And everybody knows that you have a temper, too. Those animals would have to watch out."

She giggled. "I wish I didn't have to learn all these girl things. If they would let me, I'll bet I could do all the things that boys do. That would be more fun than growing vegetables and weaving cotton."

"The things we do are not really so much fun like you think. After listening to the story today, I have decided to be a trader. Their lives are hard and dangerous, but they get to go to lots of places."

"Girls can be traders, too," she said. "Maybe I will be one so we can be together. I would like that."

"I would like it, too," he said.

I truly hope we can both be traders and visit new places and meet new people together. He chuckled inwardly. *It is strange, but I have never mentioned taking Aiyana as a wife when we come of age and neither has she mentioned it, and yet we know that it will happen. Our families know, too.*

"Come on," she said. "I'll race you to the beach for a swim."

~~*~~

Just weeks after the session with the storyteller, the Carib struck. A little past sunup, Anoki was with a party just leaving for a fishing trip. The party was out to sea, but Boriken was still in sight. Anoki glanced toward the island and saw some activity on the shoreline.

He pointed toward the activity. "What's going on there?" He asked. Is that another fishing party?"

The man next to him looked in the direction he was pointing. "No, boy, we are the only fishing party for today, and look, that is far too many people for a fishing trip." He shaded his eyes with his hand. "That is the Carib. They are raiding our village. We must turn back!"

They turned the prows of their canoes toward Boriken.

As they were landing their canoes they could see that they were too late to help, for the Carib were already leaving.

The relatively small group of Carib warriors were making their way to their canoes. Most of The men in the fishing party of sixteen men had weapons, but since it appeared that the Carib had finished their raid and were now withdrawing, they took no action. The kaseek Guaraca did not allow pursuit of raiders; it was strictly forbidden. The Carib raiders, who were likely also aware of that policy, made no attempt to attack the fishing party.

They saw that the raiders had taken a few captives, but it would even be forbidden to try to rescue them.

As Anoki watched, one of the captives managed to pull free from her captor and ran toward the fishing party. But she slipped and fell as the man pursued her. Anoki saw that she was a young girl. She was plump, and perhaps a little older than Aiyana. The man grabbed her by the arm and roughly pulled her up.

Anoki was angered, but frustrated that he had no way to help her. He spotted a small rock on the ground and picked it up. He hurled it with all his might at the Carib. The rock caught the man on the side of his head just above the ear, knocking him down.

As the Carib fell, the girl got up and ran toward the village. Anoki did not get a clear look at the plump girl's face as she fled.

The man recovered, got up, and started toward Anoki, who decided it would be wiser to retreat rather than face the man. As he turned to run, he heard a yell coming from one of the Carib in the canoes calling to the man. The Carib cursed Anoki and ran toward the canoes.

Anoki then sped toward the village.

~~*~~

He knew that something was wrong as soon as he entered the bohio. Aiyana's mother and father were holding each other and weeping, and both were being consoled by Anoki's mother.

He went to them. "What is it...what's the matter?"

"They've taken Aiyana," his mother told him, "and they've killed Adahi, her oldest brother. Her father tried to stop them, but one of them clubbed him. But luckily it was a glancing blow and just stunned him."

Anoki spotted a spear still in the rack. He rushed to the rack and grabbed it. "I'm going after her," he said. "I will bring her back or die trying."

"No," his mother said. "They will just kill you, too. You are still just a boy, but even if you were a grown man you could do nothing."

"I don't care. If I die it doesn't matter if Aiyana is in their hands."

Aiyana's father, Akajuju, spoke up. "Your mother is right, Anoki. You will do nothing but get yourself killed. I have lost my daughter and my eldest son, and believe me if I thought there was a way I could avenge my son and bring my daughter back, I would surely do it."

"But I want her to know that I at least tried."

"She would never know. They will kill you before you get near her. I would go with you if I thought there was even the slightest chance to rescue her. But how could we even find her? The Carib inhabit many islands, and we don't even know which island the raiders came from. Another thing to consider is that Guaraca prohibits following them or counter attacking. He could order your death for disobeying."

Anoki hung his head and sobbed in grief. "You are right," he said. "But maybe we can petition the kaseek to change his mind. Maybe he will let some of us organize a force of our own, separate from the kaseek's command. We could conduct raids of our own and pay the Carib back for the misery they have caused us. We never strike back.

If we started retaliating with our own raids they will not be so eager to attack us."

"Guaraca would never allow it," said Akajuju, "and even if he did we could not match the Carib. They teach warfare to their people from childhood and it becomes a way of life with them. They are far more skillful with weapons than the Taino.

"Our own kaseek, as the other kaseeks, want to keep things the way they are."

"There must be a way," said Anoki. "I will find a way."

Anoki could see that things were hopeless, but a part of him still retained a spark of hope. He went to his hammock and lay down. He felt utterly dejected, as if fate itself was plotting against him.

There must be something that I can do. If things are hopeless here, maybe I could run away. Maybe I could even join the Carib and pretend to be one of them until I could find Aiyana. And then we could sneak away from them.

But one horrible thought was in the back of his mind. *They keep the women captives for their wives, but they are known to sometimes eat their enemies. What if they...* He pushed the thought from his mind; he did not even want to think about it.

~~*~~

Aiyana lay in the rear of the canoe, her hands and feet tied with cotton strands. Her upper thigh rested on the sharp edge of a broken conch shell that was rubbing her skin raw. It was painful, but she would not complain to her captors. She would not ask any favor of them, even if she were dying.

She raised her head and could see about twenty Carib warriors; it was a fairly large canoe. She saw that she was the only captive in this canoe. She knew that the Carib had taken five more, all girls about her age. *The other girls must be in different canoes; I wonder what they are going to do with us.*

She looked at the sweaty back of the rowing Carib directly in front of her.

"If you are going to eat me I hope that you choke to death on my flesh."

He turned his head and stared at her. "Be quiet, girl. You are to become my wife." He sneered and grunted. "We don't eat weaklings like you. We take in the strong and brave to gain strength in our own bodies." He laughed. "You might make a tasty morsel, though." He turned and continued to row.

She noticed that the Carib's words were spoken in Arawak, but although heavily accented she had no trouble understanding him.

He means to take me for a wife. Ha. I would rather be killed and eaten.   I have heard that they like Taino wives and that they have taken many.

She raised her head again and peered over the side of the canoe. She could still see Boriken but it was growing farther and farther away.

I will never see Boriken again. I will never see my family...or Anoki again. I want to die. The Carib is not looking; perhaps I can work myself over the side of the canoe and fall into the sea. I will be sure to drown because my hands and feet are bound.

Ever so slowly she began inching her way toward the side of the canoe. She raised her head and shoulders and lifted her chin so that it rested on the top edge of the canoe's side. She drew her knees up and pushed with her feet, while at the same time she pressed her chin downward so that her body slid backward and upward. Her movement caused the conch edge to bite deeper into her leg. Though she had managed to pull clear of the conch now, she could feel blood oozing from the wound.

I must be careful not to rock the canoe until I am going over the side. Then they will be unable to stop me.

Her legs were now straightened and she once more drew her knees up and pushed with her feet. Her breasts and shoulders were now above the top edge of the canoe.

She glanced at the Carib. *Please, please don't look back now.*

She had now positioned herself so that she was sitting upright. She drew her knees up once more. *One more hard push with my feet and a strong twist of my body should send me overboard.*

~~*~~

Anoki lay on his hammock, planning his escape. *I will have to steal a canoe, and since all canoes are the property of the kaseek, I will surely be put to death if I am caught. But I will have to take a chance.*

His thoughts were interrupted. Akajuju approached his hammock. "I think I know what you are planning, Anoki. Please don't do anything foolish like running away from the village, for it will only get you in trouble."

Anoki looked at him. "Akajuju, I respect you, and you have been like a father to me, but I must do what I must do."

"I know how you feel for my grief is deep, too, and as I have said, if I thought there was any chance at all I would go with you. We can take some small consolation that Aiyana is probably still alive, for the Carib usually take Taino girls for their wives."

"That she is probably still alive gives me all the more reason to go and look for her."

"You cannot see it, but that would be near impossible. I am confident that you have learned navigation well enough to find your way to the Carib's islands, but you must remember that they occupy many islands. You would have no way of finding Aiyana."

Before Anoki could answer, Mahala, one of Kaseek Guaraca's deputies entered the Bohio.

"Is Anoki here?" She asked.

Anoki arose from the hammock. "Yes. I am here."

"Please come with me; Guaraca wishes to see you."

"What...what does he want?"

"He didn't say, he just sent me to get you."

He followed her out the door. *Is it possible he somehow knows I was planning to run away? But how could he know? His priest, the boheek, is said to have magical powers. Could he know what I was planning?*

Or maybe he thinks that I pursued the Carib when I helped the girl.

He started preparing a defense in case the kaseek accused him of pursuit. *I did not pursue them; I merely helped the girl to escape. The raiders did not come after me when I helped the girl, so even they did not consider it an attack.*

The boheek, with his magical powers, will know that my innermost intentions were good.

They reached Guaraca's Kaney and Mahala led him in. Guaraca was sitting on his dujo, meaning he was to greet someone of importance, as a kaseek from a chiefdom, or to view a ceremony or game at the batey.

Is he going to sentence me to death? Surely he couldn't have me put to death for helping the girl to escape.

Guaraca motioned him forward. Anoki approached him and stood before him. The Kaseek was an elderly man, lighter-skinned than most Taino, mainly from staying in his kaney much of the time. He was wearing his formal headdress, a brightly colored headband with a plumage of feathers rising above his forehead. His graying hair flowed from the band down to his shoulders. His ornate necklace, waistband, and knee length loincloth gave him an imposing appearance.

"Anoki, I have summoned you here to thank you for saving my eldest daughter. I learned who you were from a member of your fishing party, Shoja, who is a brother of my number one wife.

His daughter! I thought she looked familiar even though I didn't see her face.

My daughter tells me that you were very brave to face a Carib warrior, and to fell him with a rock, giving her time to escape. I am indebted to you, and if anytime I can do something for you just let me know."

Anoki cleared his throat. "Most High, there is something I would ask of you right now."

The kaseek looked a little surprised. "Yes, what do you wish?"

"During the raid the Carib captured my wife-to-be, Aiyana, and killed her brother. It is my wish to go after her. I ask you for permission to go and also for a small canoe."

Guaraca was shocked by the request. "Do you realize what you ask of me? I have a strict policy of not following them after a raid. We fight to defend ourselves when they

64

attack but never do we counter attack. It is better to lose a few of our people in these raids than to wage a bloody war with them.

"Anoki, you are a boy, though you are becoming a man. How can you hope to rescue Aiyana? What you plan to do is impossible. Are you aware of the futility of such a venture?

"Yes, Most High, I am aware, but I am willing to risk even my life if I must. Without Aiyana my life would seem worthless. I know that I may never return, and I accept that. But I feel that I must at least try."

Guaraca thought for a period, a period that seemed a lifetime to Anoki. He finally answered. "Very well. I promised you a favor so I will give you permission. You may take a small two-man canoe and whatever supplies you wish. But you must go alone. The Carib should not feel motivated for vengeance if only one young man follows. But you must promise me that if you are captured, you will tell them you ran away, and not tell them I gave you permission."

"I give you my word, Great Chief."

" I assume you will leave as soon as possible."

"Yes. They already have a good head start. I will leave as soon as possible.

I will have the boheek bless you before you leave.

~~*~~

He loaded water, food supplies, and a spear into the canoe. It was late morning when he left. He rowed eastward hugging the coast of Boriken until he reached the eastern end of the island, and then turned the prow of the little canoe to head in a southeasterly direction.

The sea is calm and the wind is with me. Yakahu has been good to me so far.

Anoki rowed with determination. At this point his only goal was to move forward toward his destination. He had no idea what he would do once he reached his goal. He wasn't even thinking about it. He only knew that he must reach the islands of the Carib, and that he must find Aiyana.

The sun had reached its high point overhead and was now descending. He pulled in his oars, and ate and drank while he rested.

Feeling refreshed, he continued his journey.

~~*~~

Aiyana had the upper part of her body over the edge of the canoe, but just as she was trying to push with her feet and wriggle over the side, the canoe rocked. The Carib turned around and made a grab for her. He had her in his grasp before she could slip over the side. He pulled her back in and roughly pushed her down. This time she was face down.

The Carib spoke gruffly in his heavy accent. "You would kill yourself before becoming the wife of a Carib?"

"Yes. I would rather be food for the sharks. I hate you."

"Ha. You are not meek and submissive like most of our Taino women. You show bravery and spirit. Perhaps your flesh would be better to feed my spirit than to be a wife. I will think on it."

"I will never willingly be your wife. Never."

One of the Carib called back from the other end of the canoe. "What is going on back there?

"This one does not wish to be a wife. I will barbeque her flesh instead."

The Carib grunted, then returned to his rowing.

Now that she was lying on her stomach, the conch shell was cutting in to the front part of her thigh. It was getting more painful. *Perhaps if I can reach down with my hands I can push the shell away from my body.*

She reached down with her bound hands and found the conch. *Why am I concerned about a shell cutting into my skin when they will be roasting my flesh in a day or two.*

As she started moving the conch shell, an idea came to her. *The shell! It is probably sharp enough to cut the cotton binding.*

Instead of moving the conch, she moved it into a position where she could rub her bonds against the jagged edge of the broken shell.

She was forced to work very slowly, as the Carib was now watching her more often. Once her hand slipped and she rubbed the sharp edge of the shell against the palm of her hand. She gritted her teeth to keep from crying out. She ignored the pain and continued.

Free! Her hands were free now. *It will be more difficult to reach my feet; I will have to be very careful.*

But she noticed that the Carib was paying less attention, probably thinking that she was under control now. She rolled over, ever so lightly, on her side. It was awkward reaching down to her ankles, but her fingers found the cotton strands binding her feet.

She was startled to find that the binding around her feet was loose. *I can't believe it. It is almost loose enough to push from my ankles. It must have come loose as I was pushing with my feet. Yakahu is surely with me.*

She waited until the Carib turned to check on her, careful to keep her hands together, and then once more reached down to her feet. Another push against the strand and she felt it sliding down. She pulled her hands back up now, feeling sure she could work the bonds off by movement of her feet.

She kept her hands together with the cotton strands laid across her wrists. The Carib glanced back several times, but never noticed. She caught the strand with her toe and kept moving her feet, slowly so as not to attract attention. She felt the bonds slipping farther downward until...free!

She was no longer bound, so she could pull herself up and jump out before the Carib could react. She tightened her muscles and sprang up. She could see the surprised look on her captor's face as he quickly turned. He made a grab for her, but he was too late. She dove into the sea with her arms and legs already churning the water, pulling her away from the canoe.

The saltwater at first stung her cuts from the conch shell, but now felt soothing. She was pulling farther away, but glanced back at the canoe to see that the Carib was no longer there. He had plunged into the water and was coming after her. She looked back to see that he was not far behind, perhaps two or three body lengths.

She glanced back several times to see that she was not gaining on him, but luckily he was not gaining on her, either.

We are getting farther away from the canoe. How far will he continue to pursue me?

Her question was answered in the next few moments. He stopped and began swimming back toward the canoe. But she knew that she was not safe from him yet.

Is he so determined to recapture me that he will have his friends turn the canoe around to come after me?

She looked back to see that the canoe was now too far away to tell if the man had reached it yet. She was pulling farther away with every stroke of her arms, but she still didn't feel safe.

They can still overtake me if they come after me with the canoe.

She continued her pace, and after a fairly long period nothing happened.

They must have resumed their journey back to their island. They probably thought that it was not worth it to continue pursuit, and anyway they are pretty sure that I will eventually drown. I probably will if the sharks don't get me first, but that will be better than being their captive.

She was tiring and slowed her pace, treading water for a while to rest. She continued on but at a much slower pace. She was determined to go as far as she could, and moving at a faster pace would only wear her out. The sun was low in the sky now and it would soon be dark.

~~*~~

Anoki was far out to sea now. He guessed that it not long until he reached the islands of the Carib. He was now beginning to think about what he would do once he arrived at his destination. He had once thought of telling them that he wished to become a Carib and pretend to join them, but the more he thought of that idea the less he liked it.

They will probably not accept me, and see me only as an enemy. Even if they did accept me, they would expect me to conform to their ways. I would be expected to accompany them on raids and to attack my own people. I could never do that. But I have come this far, so I must do something.

Guaraca made me promise that if captured I would not disclose that he gave me permission to come. I have nothing to identify me as a Taino, so maybe I will also not disclose that I am from Boriken. I could tell them that I am an Arawak from the Orinoco that got lost. If they ask me to tell what the Orinoco is like, I will tell them of the jungles, great rivers, fierce animals and snakes.

He made his decision; that's what he would tell them. He had to have some reason to explain why he was here, and he could think of nothing better. But what if the Carib also considered the Arawak as their enemies? He would just have to take that chance.

He looked to the west to see that the sun was now touching the horizon. It would be dark soon, but he would be able to continue his southeastern course as he had learned to read the stars.

It was almost dusk when his peripheral vision picked up an object in the water to the east. It was just a speck, and he took it to be a piece of driftwood. But as he kept looking he thought he saw movement. He knew that the eye could be fooled into seeing movement when staring at distant objects, particularly in dim light.

He would not waste his energy or be deterred from his goal by chasing after driftwood. He kept rowing, but he glanced at the object again. This time he was sure it was moving. His curiosity got the best of him and he turned toward the object.

As he drew nearer he could see that it was definitely moving.

By the three demons! Is that a person? What would anyone be doing swimming here in the open sea?

But he could now see that whoever it was, was swimming away from him and trying to evade him. He continued to get closer as he rowed, while at the same time he shouted out.

"Hello! I mean no harm to you. I want to help you."

The figure immediately stopped, turned, and came toward him.

He was shocked and dumbfounded, and at the same time overjoyed. It was Aiyana!

He pulled her into the canoe and they embraced. For the first few moments they said nothing, but just held each other tight as she was catching her breath.

Anoki became conscious of the touch of her body, her breasts against his. *This is the first time ever that we have held each other like this.*

Aiyana, still catching her breath, was the first to speak. "I...I thought I would never see you again."

He held her tighter. "And I felt the same. But I followed, even though everyone thought it was futile."

"At first I thought you were my captor coming after me, but when I heard your voice calling I was elated; I almost couldn't believe it. It was too good to be true."

She caught her breath and was breathing normal now. She asked for water. He gave her the water and they shared dried fruits as he told her of what had taken place after the raid. She in turn told him of her capture and escape.

"I don't think I could have lasted much longer in the water. I was getting very tired."

He looked at her wounds from the broken conch shell. "There is no bleeding, but some raw flesh still shows. We will have to wait until we get back to the village, and then the boheek can treat the wounds with his magical herbs."

"It doesn't hurt at all. I'm sure it will heal without the boheek's herbs."

They finished their meal and set out for Boriken.

Back to top

Return to Boriken

Even before they landed the canoe, the people of the chiefdom were greeting them at the beach. Akajuju was among the first to greet them and he shed tears of joy as he held his daughter. When the villagers learned of what had happened, they hailed both Anoki and Aiyana as heroes. Never before had anyone succeeded in escaping the Carib once captured.

Guaraca summoned both of them. He did not have them brought to his kaney, but met them at the batey field. He did not need to summon all the people of his chiefdom, for they were already flocking to the field.

The kaseek, in full regalia, was carried to the field in his sedan chair. His attendants placed a small platform on one end of the field and set the kaseek's dujo upon it. The kaseek mounted the platform and seated himself on the dujo. The boheek and a deputy mounted the platform and stood behind the kaseek.

Anoki and Aiyana stood in a cleared area directly in front of the platform.

"Anoki and Aiyana, everyone is happy for your safe return and we are all proud of you for escaping the Carib. I congratulate both of you for your courageous actions. Aiyana, you did not meekly submit to the Carib, but fought them. You outwitted them and made good your escape.

"Anoki, in spite of all the obstacles hindering you, with your determination and perseverance you overcame them and went to Aiyana's rescue.

72

"I commend you both for your heroic deeds. And now the boheek will bless you.

The boheek stepped down. Anoki and Aiyana kneeled as the boheek chanted his blessing.

When the boheek finished, Guaraca addressed the crowd.

"My people, the deeds of Anoki and Aiyana were admirable, and they deserve praise. But we all must remember that this was a very special case. Nothing like this has ever happened before and will not likely ever happen again. I gave Anoki permission to follow them only because he rescued my daughter."

He continued. "The Carib certainly will not see the escape of a Taino captive as a Taino counter attack, but will consider it merely the actions of one individual. They were not aware of the actions of Anoki at all, so we needn't fear reprisal from them because of this event.

"But remember that my command to not pursue the Carib after a raid remains in effect. To pursue and counter attack will only invite them to declare all out war against us. This would disrupt our peaceful way of life that we have enjoyed for so many years.

"We will continue to resist them to the best of our ability during a raid of our village, but once they withdraw we must not pursue them.

"I thank you all for your attendance, and now the boheek will bless us all."

After the blessing the crowd broke up.

~~*~~

A year passed and very soon Anoki and Aiyana would come of age to marry, and after that they would request to be assigned as traders. Anoki's mother had hoped that he would become a canoe maker, and thus remain near home. The canoe makers did not even have to fish or hunt. But Anoki was the adventurous type, and chose trading.

They were certain they would be granted the trading assignment, as they had remained in good favor with Guaraca and his court. And also Guaraca presently had no traders in his chiefdom. The last group of traders from the chiefdom had left for a trip and never returned. It was assumed that they perished in a storm, or perhaps they had met up with Calusa warriors from the land of Bimini who sometimes preyed upon traders.

But for now Anoki and Aiyana were still considered in training, even though in reality they were performing the same tasks that the adults were performing.

On most days they were kept apart, performing different kinds of tasks, but during the heat of the day they were allowed to rest or participate in recreational activities. One day they were swimming when a group of traders arrived. Anoki and Aiyana were excited for two reasons. It was fascinating to see what new types of goods the traders would bring, and they could also ask questions of the traders, since trading was the line of work that they would be doing in only a matter of days.

They went to greet the traders and found that they had come from Kuba, a large island to their west. The traders spoke Arawak, but with a slightly different accent.

The items they offered were the usual trinkets, jewelry, pottery, and cloth. But their wares had designs unique to kuba, and many were beautiful and colorful. Some of their items were made from snake or crocodile skins.

News of the traders quickly spread, and before long the Kubans had traded all their wares and taken in items from Boriken. As the traders were preparing to go, Anoki and Aiyana approached them. One of the four greeted them.

"Welcome to you, but we are sorry to tell you that we have traded all our wares, and we have nothing left."

"We don't wish to trade anything, but only want to ask a few questions. We plan to become traders in the next few days, and would like to ask whatever advice you might have for us," said Anoki.

"There is not much to say," said the trader, "We make sure that our canoes are sturdy, and large enough to hold our wares. Be honest, for people will remember if you are not." He laughed. "At the same time don't be gullible. And be prepared for hardships and many days away from your people. There is not much more to say"

"We expect hardships," said Aiyana. "But I imagine you see some interesting things during your trips"

The trader chuckled. "It may not be as interesting as you think. But recently we did come upon a strange situation in Kiskeya. A strange group of men in giant canoes were there. The people there had nothing to offer for trading with us, for they had traded gifts with the strange men. But the strange men came to our canoe to trade and had items such as we have never seen. They gave us some of their items but did not demand many of our items in return. We still had nearly all of our wares so we came here to trade.

"Who were they? Where did they come from?" Anoki asked.

"We never found out. But it was a distant land in the east. They were strange indeed. They wore cloth that covered their entire body, some had metal covering their heads, and they allowed the hair to grow on their face."

Anoki was fascinated, and hoped to see these strange men himself.

~~*~~

On to Kiskeya

The kaseek joined them in marriage and the boheek blessed them. Aiyanna donned the cloth that covered her pubic area, which would identify her as a married woman. They were granted two days free of work assignments.

Immediately after the two day period they approached Mahala, the kaseek's deputy, who was responsible for assignments and requested to be given the job as traders. They had already told Mahala of their wishes, and she immediately made it official that they would be Guaraca's traders.

"Takoda and Tehya, another recently married couple, will make up the team."

Anoki and Aiyana were not surprised, for they knew the couple and knew of their wish to become traders. The couple had gone through much of the training with Anoki and Aiyana. Takoda was a tall, slim young man, good natured but serious; Tehya was a short, petite girl, who was outgoing and bouncy. As different as they were in personalities, they adored each other.

Mahala called the four of them together and briefed them on their duties. "In the past we have traded with people in villages along the coasts of Kiskeya, Kuba, Matakumbe, Bahama, Jamaika, and Bimini. You may seek out new trading partners, but be careful that you do not stray too far. That may be the reason why the previous trading crew did not return.

76

"In all these places except Bimini they speak Arawak, but you will always find someone there who can speak enough Arawak to make trades."

Anoki spoke up. "I would like for our first trading trip to be Kiskeya if that is alright with you."

"I can see no reason why not. You may prepare to leave whenever you are ready.

Mahala collected items from artisans of the village such as wood carved figurines, sculpted stone figures, pottery, and body ornaments such as necklaces, bracelets, and anklets of gold, bone, and brightly colored shells.

They chose a canoe as advised by the Kubans. It was long enough and wide enough to hold their wares, yet it was small enough for four to row easily'...and two could row if necessary.

It was wide, being dugout from one of the wider tabonuco trees. There was also space enough for two to sleep.

~~*~~

As they rowed westward, the four discussed the strange men that the Kuban traders had spoken of.

"I would like to see them for myself," said Anoki. "It has been nearly two moons, but I am hoping they are still there. The traders did not tell us very much about them, and I would like to learn more."

"But they are most likely gone by now," said Aiyana. "If they were traders, they will be looking for other places."

Tehya giggled. "Wouldn't it be funny if they were to visit Boriken while we are visiting Kiskeya? Anoki, don't turn this canoe around and go back now because of what I said." She laughed again. "I'll bet that's what you're thinking."

Anoki laughed. "I would like very much to see them, but I promise I won't turn the canoe around. And anyway we would probably have met them if they were going to Boriken."

"It would be interesting to meet those men," said Takoda, "But we must remember that the main reason for our trip is for trading."

Tehya playfully punched him. "Old meanie."

Everyone laughed, including Takoda.

At nightfall they took turns rowing; two rowed while two slept.

~~*~~

They reached Kiskeya on the third dawn since leaving, and rowed their canoe along the shoreline until they caught sight of the giant canoes of the Spaniards. They were on the western end of the island.

"They are still here," said Anoki. "Now we can meet them."

They arrived at the landing point in a cove and beached their canoe. A short time later people began gathering, and soon people were bargaining for their wares. They had traded most of their wares, and only a few stragglers were still there. Anoki spoke to one of them.

"We have heard of the strange men here and we see two of their canoes, but we have seen none of them here. We are curious why they do not come."

"They are getting ready to leave," an elderly woman replied. "But they will come back. A few of them will remain here, and they have built their own settlement.

They have told us that the craft they have are not canoes. They call them ships." She paused, then added, "They call themselves Spaniards."

"Why will some of them stay behind?" Asked Takoda.

"One of their ships went into water that was too shallow and they could not move it out. They did not have enough room on two ships to take all the men back with them, they said."

She had no sooner spoken than Anoki spotted five of the men coming from the ship in a strange looking canoe. They had a villager with them. The men landed and got out. Anoki was examining the boat.

He looked at the villager who had come with them. "What kind of canoe is this?"

"They don't call it a canoe, they call it a boat," answered the villager. "I am Shilah, of the territory of Kaseek Guacanagari, and I speak for the Spaniards.

The men eyed Anoki's canoe and said something in a strange language.

"He is a deputy chief of his people," said Shilah. "He says you have good wares for trade, but he didn't bring anything with him to trade."

"Most of what is in the canoe is what we received in trade from the villagers here," said Anoki, "and is not for trade. But I have heard the men are going to their homeland and will return. Tell the Spaniard that when he returns, perhaps we can trade."

The interpreter spoke to the man, who made a reply. "He says perhaps so," Shilah said, "but now he must go to retrieve a few items and return to his ship." The Spaniards turned and headed inland, followed by Shilah.

"Before we leave for Boriken, I would love some fresh fruit," said Tehya. "I'm tired of dried fruit all the time. Can't we look around for some fruit trees?"

"We are in no hurry, so go ahead if you wish." Said Anoki'

She playfully grabbed Takoda's hand, pulling him after her. "Come on, let's look for fruit."

"I want some fruit, too," said Aiyana. "Let's all go."

"Go ahead," Anoki said, "I'll stay here and watch the canoe."

"I'll bring some back for you," she said.

~~*~~

A short while after they left, two men approached carrying a items in baskets. "I am Jumaca," said one. "I am a woodcarver and I have some of my carvings here. Do you still have some wares for trade?"

Anoki looked at his items. "Your wares are nice. We don't have many of our wares left for trading, but you can look at what we have, and maybe we will trade."

He looked at the other man. "What do you have?"

"Nothing. I have come with Jumaca."

As the men were looking at the wares, the Spaniards returned. Anoki was standing at the water's edge looking out at the ships. Two Spaniards walked up beside him. One of them pointed at their boat and said something.

"He says for you to get in the boat," said Shilah.

"I can't. I must wait for my crew to return." He turned to see that Jumaca and his friend were also being ordered to get in the boat.

Shilah frantically whispered to him. "You must not resist them or they will kill you."

Suddenly there was a commotion as Jumaca's friend bolted and ran. One of the Spaniards pointed his metal

80

stick at him. There was a loud sound like thunder from the stick, and the man dropped. Anoki was shocked to see blood oozing from a wound in the man's back. The Spaniards ordered Jumaca to drag the corpse into the water near the boat.

The Spaniards then pointed their sticks at Anoki and Jumaca and shouted at them.

"They are telling you to get in their boat. You had better do as they say or they will kill you too."

Still in a daze, Anoki and Jumaca stepped into the boat.

Shilah looked at Jumaca. "They want you to hold on to the body as they row us out of the cove, and then release the body when we are far from shore."

As they headed toward the ships, Shilah explained what was happening.

"The chief of all the Spaniards here is called Colon; his Taino name is Qualon. He has promised the great chief in his homeland to return with much wealth. The Spaniards have not told me, but I have heard them talking of taking us back to display to their people and to their great chief. They already have three others on their ship who have volunteered to go and were granted permission by Guacanagari. The Spaniards want to take more in case some of us don't survive the trip. They saw you here and decided to take you, even though they haven't consulted with the kaseek."

"Did you volunteer?" Anoki asked.

"I only volunteered because Guacanagari asked me to. Qualon requested him to have me accompany him because I am one of only three who can speak some of their language."

"Guacanagari will be angry if he finds that the Spaniards have forced me to go against my will," said Jumaca, "and even more angry that they have killed my friend."

"But how will he find out?" Shilah asked. "And even if he does find out he will probably do nothing. He seems to be afraid of Qualon."

~~*~~

It was dark down in the hold where Anoki and Jumaca were being held. Even after his eyes got used to the dark, Anoki could see the face of his fellow prisoner only dimly. It was hot, dank, and smelly in the hold. Shilah had told them that the crew would keep them here only until the ship sailed, and then they could complete the journey on the deck with the three volunteers. But for now they would keep them down here to prevent an escape attempt.

The homeland of the Spaniards is in a distant land far to the east. This minor kaseek, Qualon, wants to display us to his great kaseek like we are some kind of strange objects. He may never bring us back again. I may never see my people or my beloved Aiyana again. I must find a way to escape before we set out. I must.

It seemed a very long time before he sensed that the ship was starting to move. .

It is too late now. We are on our way to their faraway land.

~~*~~

Aiyana, Tehya, and Takoda arrived back at the canoe bringing bananas, parchas, and papayas. They were surprised to find Anoki missing. The items they had

82

received in trade from the Kiskeyans and the few items that were leftover of their own were still there. They began calling loudly for him.

"He must have wandered far off for some reason," observed Takoda. "Maybe to find fruit himself?

"No, I told him I would bring some back." She frowned. "I hope nothing has happened to him."

Tehya hugged her, "Don't worry, we will find him around somewhere. Besides, what could have happened to him?"

"If he does not come back soon," Takoda observed, "we had better go looking for him."

"I think it is time to look for him now," said Aiyana.

"Alright," said Takoda, "but one of us should stay here and watch the canoe."

"I will stay," said Aiyana, "in case he comes back to the canoe."

She was restless, and wandered about aimlessly for a long time. Afterward she grew tired and sat down and waited on a canoe that was beached and turned upside down,.

It was growing dark when they returned. "We searched a wide area around here, and asked several of the people here if they had seen him." Takoda said. "He is nowhere to be found. It is as if the magic of a boheek has made him disappear."

"I know he did not wander off, " said Aiyana. "He is not like that. Even if he did, he would not go far."

"Did he ever do anything to make the boheek angry?" Asked Tehya.

"Never," replied Aiyana. "He was well-liked by both the kaseek and the boheek. "

"We have looked for nearly half a day," Takoda said. "We haven't much choice but to return to Boriken now."

"No...no, please," Aiyana begged. "Please wait until tomorrow morning. He will return, I know it."

"Really, we should go," answered Takoda. "We work for Guaraca and the people, and we must consider them first."

Tehya spoke up. "Takoda, my love, you are right that we should look out for the kaseek and the people. But I beg you to consider this with your heart and not your logic. In the absence of Anoki you make the decisions, and must answer to Mahala when we return. But we have traded nearly all of our goods and have good wares to show for them. Surely Mahala will commend you for waiting a little longer for a fellow trader."

Takoda thought a few moments. "Yes, he said, "Anoki would do the same for me, I know. And you are right. Maybe Mahala would not approve if we left too soon without him. We will wait until tomorrow morning."

The banana tree was not too far, so they went for the leaves of the plant, which Tainos sometimes use for pallets. It was a clear night, and a crescent moon was showing as they made their beds near the canoe. As they were making the pallets, Tehya exclaimed, "Look, the Spaniards are leaving."

Aiyana looked to see that the ships had set out and were moving with the wind. *Anoki is fascinated with the Spaniards and their ships. He would love to see this.*

She lay down on her banana leave pallet, but it was a long time before she drifted off to sleep.

~~*~~

Shortly after the ship started moving, several crew members came down for the two Taino. Armed men escorted them to the upper deck. Anoki drew in a deep breath of the fresh air, glad to leave the foul air of the hold. It was already after dark when they arrived on deck, but the night was clear and many stars were visible. A crescent moon dimly lit the waters of a calm sea. They were taken to an area of the ship where the other Taino were staying. The food they were given was standard Taino diet. "The food is from our storehouses," Shilah explained. "Guacanagari gave them supplies because they were running out."

One of the Spaniards said something to Shilah. He translated, "They say that you will get two meals a day, morning and evening. You must not leave this area assigned to you because you will get in the way of the crew performing their duties. Once a day, near sunset, you will be allowed to leave your area and move around other parts of the deck for a while. When you do, you must keep together."

Their assigned space was roped off, and it was small and cramped. There was barely room for the five of them to bed down at night. They were given straw and squares of cloth for their bedding.

Shilah was quartered in a different location, but he stayed with them for a while and talked.

"You have learned their language well, said one of the group. How did you manage to learn it?"

Shilah chuckled. "I haven't learned it well, I still struggle with it. One of the Spaniards knows much about languages, and is learning our Taino language well. He taught me much about his language. He is one of them who is staying behind"

"Have you learned much of their ways?" Anoki asked.

"Some of their ways are much like ours," said Shilah, "but most are very strange. One way they differ is how we value the yellow metal. We use it only for ornaments and jewelry, but they covet it, and are always seeking to find more. It seems they can never have enough. It is as if they worship it.

"Do they worship Yakahu?" One of them asked.

"No. They have a god. They say they worship only one god, but they have some strange beliefs. I recently heard them speaking of sea monsters. They believe there are powerful and fearsome monsters living in the sea, like giant serpents."

Anoki laughed. "The most fearsome things in the sea are sharks, not serpents."

Shilah stayed and talked with them a while longer, and then returned to his quarters.

~~*~~

Three days later, in the morning they were awakened and given their meals. After three days Anoki was growing weary of the cramped space they were in, but at the same time he was fascinated with the ship. He marveled at the way the wind caught the sails, and how the sailors adjusted them for controlling the ship's direction.

He now understood why the Taino could get in their way. The crew of the ship seemed to be keeping busy with all different kinds of duties. They were working on the deck, up in the rigging, and going below deck in performing their duties. Still, he did not like the cramped area they were in, and welcomed the brief freedom they were given after the evening meals. As they moved about the deck of the ship in their free time, Anoki was getting a better view of their surroundings.

We are moving with the wind, and we are going a little faster than a canoe. We have been going since a little after sunset three days ago to nearly sunset today. We are moving to the east, so if we were traveling by canoe we would be close to reaching Boriken by sundown. Unless we have traveled slower or faster than I estimate, we should now be directly north of Boriken. Unless the ship has followed a course too far northward, we should not be too far from the island.

The sun had not yet set, and the horizon was still visible. He stopped momentarily, shaded his eyes, and scanned the southern horizon. His heart leapt to his throat, for to the south and west, barely discernible on the horizon, land was visible. It would go unnoticed unless one was looking for it.

That can only be Boriken. It is a little to the west, so that means we have passed it.

He glanced at the armed crew member who was assigned to watch them. He jumped up and down and pointed randomly at the sea, while screaming at Shilah. "I see a sea serpent!"

Shilah interpreted what he was saying, and their guard and other nearby Spaniards ran to the side to get a look.

In the confusion, Anoki ran and dove overboard. He was pulling away from the ship before his guard recovered from the surprise. The guard got off one shot, but Anoki was pulling out of range before the man could reload.

He faintly heard Shilah calling. "Come back, or you will surely drown."

I may drown, but I will die knowing I did not give up.

Thoughts of reuniting with Aiyana drove him on.

It grew dark, and he could no longer see the land that he thought was Boriken. He kept swimming in the direction of the last point that he saw the island.

What if I miss it? When I jumped from the ship, we had already passed it, but we couldn't have gone too far past it or I could not have seen it.

He knew from experience that anything in sight was within swimming distance.

I have been swimming long enough that it should be in sight by now. Maybe I should turn to go westward in case I went too far to the east.

He began to wonder if he had just imagined seeing it after all.

I wanted to see it so much that maybe my mind imagined it. But no, I know I saw it, and I can't give up hope or I may not make it.

But even as he was trying to build up his hope, he caught sight of the island in the dim moonlight. His adrenaline up now, his strokes became more powerful. He soon reached the shoreline of the island. Exhausted, he fell down on the beach and rested.

He was not sure he had reached Boriken. In the dim moonlight he did not see any features that he recognized. He could be on one of the offshore islands to the east of Boriken. Or, if the ship had bypassed Boriken far enough, he might be on one of the islands inhabited by the Carib.

I had better find out where I am. After I rest a little more, I will walk along the beach to see if I recognize anything.

But as he lay there on the beach resting from his long swim, he fell asleep.

~~*~~

Aiyana awakened, and it took a moment to realize that Anoki was not beside her. She looked to see that Takoda and Tehya were awake and rising from their bedding. She ran to Takoda.

"Takoda, please, can't we wait just a little longer?"

"I know how you feel," said Takoda, "but we can wait no longer. We have waited half of the day yesterday, and all through the night. We must go. We can only hope that Yakahu will bring him to you. And when we get back, we can ask the boheek for help."

Tears were streaming from Aiyana's eyes. "Please, please, just a little longer."

Tehya came to her and hugged her. "Takoda is right. We must go now, and perhaps the boheek can appeal to Yakahu to bring him to you."

"You two go," said Aiyana. "I will wait here for Anoki. I know he will come back."

"If he is still here in Kiskeya," said Takoda, "he will surely find his way back to Boriken."

Tehya held Aiyana's hand. "Yes, as Takoda says, Anoki will find his way to Boriken and to you. Oh, Aiyana, if you stay here you may miss him, or worse you may perish here. Please come with us."

Slowly, tears rolling down her cheeks, she numbly followed Tehya and stepped into the canoe. As they were pulling away from Kiskeya, She had to fight an urge to jump out of the canoe and swim back to the island. She finally realized that she was not doing her share. She picked up her oar and began rowing.

~~*~~

On the third day, the sun was high in the sky when they sighted their village on Boriken. A small crowd had gathered on the beach. Tehya pointed toward the crowd.

"Look, one of them has jumped in the water and is swimming toward us."

"That is strange," said Takoda. "Why would anyone be so anxious to see what we bring back?

Without much interest, Aiyana looked out o see the swimmer. But she shouted with joy as she recognized the swimmer...Anoki!

Anoki swam up to the canoe and pulled himself in. Tears streamed from Aiyana's eyes, but this time it was tears of joy. Anoki pull her close and kissed her tears.

He told them what had happened, how they forced him on the ship, how he escaped and swam to Boriken.

"I reached here last night, but was weary and fell asleep on the beach. This morning I found that I was only a short walk to the village. I waited here, expecting you would arrive this morning."

"We looked for you and waited. We didn't leave until the next morning," she said. "That is why we didn't arrive sooner."

They landed and beached the canoe. Mahala was there to greet them. She inspected the goods gained in the trade.

"You have done well in your first trading venture," she said. "I will look forward to many more from you in the future."

~~*~~

To Bimini

In the next few years the four of them visited points all over the Caribbean.

"The items we have brought back have been well received by the people of our village," said Anoki, "and

90

Mahala has told me that our village has been trading some of our wares with other villages on Boriken, and that other villagers are asking for more. She is going to give us a bigger canoe and two more people to help us. Guaraca has not only approved of this; he has ordered it."

"It is good to know that our wares can be found all over Boriken," said Takoda, "and that our Kaseek favors our work."

Anoki nodded. "Yes, his support is encouraging. I have been told that some of the best liked items are the furs and skins from Bimini. I will ask Mahala to send us there for our next mission."

"It is a long trip," said Anoki, "but worth it. It will take many days, even more than a moon phase."

Tehya giggled. "I don't mind. We can stop for food and water in many interesting places." She looked at Takoda. "And I know we will be back before our little one is due."

Takoda chuckled, a rarity for him, and gently rubbed her belly. "We have plenty of time. Our little one is just beginning to show."

Aiyana pulled Anoki close and whispered in his ear. Anoki smiled broadly and hugged her.

"Aiyana tells me we are going to have a little one, too."

~~*~~

The two men assigned by Mahala, Koji and Nubika, were both older men but were still good oarsmen. The crew of six prepared for the journey.

The trip going to Bimini was uneventful. They chose to trade with the Tequesta, one of the most peaceful people of Bimini. Their carvings, pottery, shell ornaments, and gold jewelry were prized by the Tequesta people, and the Taino acquired furs, skins, and other items from them to carry back to their people.

Before departing, the Tequestans gave them a gift of dried meat to eat on their journey home. The Tequestans told them that all the meat came from one animal. They found that hard to believe since no animal of that size existed on Boriken, but some of the skins and furs they received also came from large animals. On their way back they traveled southward hugging the coast of Bimini, rowing through the waterway between the outer islands and the mainland.

"The meat is good," said Tehya, "but I would like some fresh fruit, too. Can we stop along the shore and look for fruit before we leave Bimini?"

Takoda chuckled. "My dear wife loves fresh fruit."

"Me too," said Aiyana.

Anoki laughed. "My dear wife does, too. Well, we have a long trip ahead of us, so we could use some fruit during the journey."

They turned the canoe toward shore. They beached the canoe, and as they were starting to go inland to look for fruit trees, the crew was startled by a deafening roar. Anoki turned to see a huge animal emerging from the brush a short way up the beach from their location. Spear-like projections were growing from its head. It stopped momentarily and looked at them, then turned and ran away at a high rate of speed.

As the six of them looked on in amazement at the animal, the likes of which they had never seen before, another huge animal exploded from the brush. It made to give chase to the other animal, but stopped and turned to face the crew. It reared up on its hind legs, becoming taller than a man and bellowed.

"Quick, everybody to the canoe. Hurry!" Shouted Anoki.

Everybody was already rushing to the canoe, but Koji, one of the helpers assigned by Mahala, tripped over a piece of driftwood and the creature was immediately upon him.

Anoki grabbed an oar and sped to Koji's aid, followed by the others. With the five of them pounding on the animal with their oars, it gave up and retreated into the brush.

Koji, however, was badly injured; his left arm was mangled and bloody. He was still bleeding, and as they had no cotton cloth with them except their naguas and loin cloths, they used Koji's loin cloth to wash and compress his wound.

They cleaned the wound with seawater and stopped the bleeding, but Koji's arm was now useless.

"I could not believe the Tequestans even after seeing the skins," said Takoda, "but now we have seen such animals with our own eyes."

Anoki nodded. "Yes, and Chaska the story teller told of such animals in the land to the south." He paused. "We will stop at one of the islands on our way and look for fruit."

~~*~~

The rest of the trip was uneventful, but they were in for a surprise when they returned to Boriken. Mahala told of a visit by the Spaniards while they were gone.

Anoki was troubled, for he remembered his experience with the Spaniards. "I was hoping they would stay away from Boriken. They have brought misery to Kiskeya after they were welcomed there by Guacanagari. We should resist them, not welcome them."

"The Spaniards have already been welcomed," replied Mahala. "The chief Kaseek of Boriken, Agueybana, welcomed their chief, a man called Ponce de Leon. Agueybana became friends with him and gave him the Taino name of Gualeon.

"The Spaniard only asked of the kaseek to explore the island for a few days, and Agueybana granted permission. After a few days Gualeon left, and he has not been back."

"Still, I do not trust Spaniards," said Anoki.

The situation on neighboring Kiskeya worsened. Anoki and his crew no longer visited any part of the large island. Before long, all of the other traders in the Caribbean were avoiding the island. Word of the greed and cruelty of the Spaniards spread out through the region.

~~*~~

Anoki and his crew enjoyed their work and were living a peaceful and contented life. Koji's arm, with the help of the boheek, was healed and as good as new. When the time came, Aiyana and Tehya were placed in the care of Mika, the midwife. They gave birth, only days apart. After the birth of the babies, the traders were planning another trip when Mahala brought news of another visit by Gualeon.

"This time he requested to build a small settlement on Boriken, and Agueybana granted permission."

Anoki was angry. "The Spaniards will destroy us, just as they destroyed the people of Kiskeya."

"It will not be the same here as it was in Kiskeya," Mahala countered. "I was at their meeting along with other aides. Agueybana and Gualeon were very friendly with each other, and there were no disputes. But

94

Agueybana was firm in his dealings with the Spaniard. He let Gualeon know that he valued his friendship, but would not weaken as Guacanagari did.   Gualeon said that he understood and respected him for that.

"He also said that he has ordered his men to maintain goodwill and friendly relations with the Taino."

"Agueybana is a strong and respected Kaseek," said Anoki, "perhaps he will not allow the Spaniards to do as they have done in Kiskeya."

"You have no need to worry," Mahala assured him, "I know that Agueybana has issued orders to the twenty kaseeks on Boriken to resist the Spaniards if they show signs of aggression."

"I heard that when Gualeon was here before, he gave gifts to people who could find gold in the streams for him," said Tehya.

"It may be that they seek nothing but the yellow metal," said Anoki, "but after seeing what they have done in Kiskeya I am worried."

Aiyana nodded in Agreement. "I hope that Guaraca does not give them permission to enter our village."

"He will have no choice," said Anoki. "He cannot go against an order of Agueybana and risk his anger.   If Agueybana gives them permission they can enter any village they choose. None of the twenty sub-kaseeks of the island can deny them."

"Our only hope, then, is that the Spaniards will not come in numbers." Said Takoda.

Things remained peaceful on Boriken, and it appeared that Agueybana and Gualeon had become friends and gained each other's trust.

Later, Anoki learned that Gualeon had completed construction of his settlement and named it Caparra.

They say that the great kaseek in Gualeon's homeland has appointed Gualeon as the kaseek of Boriken, and that Agueybana has permitted it because Gualeon will only rule his own people at the settlement.

Though Gualeon had fifty soldiers among the settlers at Caparra, he made no aggressive moves against Agueybana's people, nor did he try to enslave the people as the Spaniards had done on Kiskeya.

Anoki's concern lessened a bit. *I am encouraged by the actions of the man called Gualeon. Perhaps Boriken will not suffer the same fate as Kiskeya.*

~~*~~

After returning from another trading venture, the crew was greeted with bad news.

"Gualeon is no longer ruling the Spaniards at Caparra," Mahala informed them. The great kaseek in his homeland has removed him and appointed another to take his place. The new ruler has not befriended Agueybana, but Agueybana stays firm in dealing with him.

"Everyone is now speaking of the greatness of Agueybana. He remains on friendly terms with the Spaniards, but does not bow to them."

Still, Anoki was skeptical. *Agueybana is strong, but I have seen the cruelty and the power of the Spaniards. I hope that Agueybana can keep Boriken from suffering the same fate as Kiskeya.*

But Anoki would learn that was not to be. He, his family, his crew, and a handful of others would survive, but Boriken would suffer the same fate as Kiskeya.

~~*~~

Epilogue

Agueybana worked to keep peace with Ponce de Leon's successors, but shortly after that he died. His brother, Agueybana II, did not trust the Spaniards. He attacked them, intending to drive them out of Boriken, but was killed in the first battle.

After the departure of Ponce de Leon, and the deaths of Agueybana and Agueybana II, things deteriorated, and soon Boriken was suffering the same fate as all the other Tainos in the Caribbean.

Boriken was in disarray, but one of the kaseeks, Mabodamaca, refused to submit and continued to fight the Spaniards. He fought hit-and-run guerilla tactics against them.

Anoki, upon hearing of the resistance of Mabodamaca, set out to join his forces. Mabodamaca fought valiantly, and his harassing tactics caused the Spaniards much distress. But eventually he was forced to retreat into the mountains of the interior. Anoki's crew followed with their children. There, in the mountains and caves they survived, along with the other Tainos who came there, for the Tainos knew the terrain of the island, and knew how to live off the land.

The End

Glossary

Agueybana..................The kaseek who befriended Ponce de Leon

Agueybana II................Brother of Agueybana

Batey.........................A Taino playing field

Bimini.......................Taino word for what is now Florida.

Boriken.....................Taino word for what is now Puerto Rico

Boheek (or bohique)......................A Taino Shaman, priest

Bohio........................A Taino dwelling

Cristobal Colon............Spanish for Christopher Columbus

Kaney........................The chief's dwelling

Kuba.........................Taino word for Cuba

Kiskeya ....Taino word for what is now Hispanola

Kaseek (or cacique)......................A Taino Chief

Gualeon................Taino for Juan Ponce de Leon

Quolon......................Taino for Christopher Columbus

The Captain General......Title of Christopher Columbus

About the Taino

It is sad that the Taino are not much more than a footnote in the history of the discovery of America. In most history books little more is said than that Columbus found Indians when he landed and gave them trinkets.

Those "Indians" were the Taino people, who warmly welcomed Columbus to their island that they called Kiskeya. Though it already had a name and was settled by the Taino, Columbus named the island Hispaniola and claimed it as a possession of the King and queen of Spain.

The Taino provided valuable aid to Columbus and his men. The local cacique, or chief, named Guacanagari, saw to it that Columbus was supplied with fresh supplies of food and water. The Taino were able to give them abundant supplies because they were proficient at farming and fishing. They kept a large storehouse filled with food at all times.

Columbus was lucky that he was dealing with the peaceful Taino. There was another people, called the Carib, inhabiting nearby islands in the Caribbean. The Carib were fierce, warlike people, who raided the Taino villages from time to time to take young women as their wives. They were also cannibalistic, and would sometimes take plump young boys during their raids.

Had Columbus first encountered the Carib, they might have slaughtered the Spaniards, which would have changed the course of history. The Spaniards had superior arms, but they would have been up against odds of more than a hundred to one.

When the Santa Maria grounded and wrecked on a sandbar, the cacique ordered his people to retrieve all the cargo for the Spaniards. When Columbus requested that the ship's timbers be brought ashore, the Taino complied. The cacique also granted Columbus permission to use the timbers to construct a fortress on Taino territory. Columbus called the fortress "La Navidad" because the event took place during Christmas.

With only two ships left, there was not enough room to take all the men back to Spain, so Columbus left thirty-nine men behind to man La Navidad. From that point on, relations between the Taino and Spaniards started to sour.

Because the Taino were a peaceful and relatively meek people, the Spaniards at La Navidad started to bully them. They got drunk, raped women, and took several women each to keep at La Navidad for their pleasure.

There are several versions of what happened while Columbus was away in Spain. The men at La Navidad were all killed. There was a neighboring cacique, named Caonabo, who was not as peaceful as Guacanagari who had befriended Columbus. Some say the Spaniards invaded Caonabo's territory to cause mischief, prompting Caonabo to strike back. Some think it was Guacanagari's own people, who were fed up with the bullying Spaniards.

Guacanagari told Columbus that Caonabo, a Carib, was responsible for the attack.

Columbus, who had returned from Spain with a much larger force, attacked Caonabo's people and chased them into the hills. But he didn't stop there. He had promised the queen that his trips would be profitable for Spain. He ordered that all the caciques pay tribute to Spain. The Spaniards took every piece of gold that they could find, and ordered all Taino people to bring them gold. Those who brought no gold were punished, sometimes by having their hands chopped off.

Some of the caciques allied against the Spaniards, but with little success. The Spaniards, with their superior arms, horses, and war dogs, killed large numbers of the Taino. Also the Spaniards brought diseases for which the Taino had no immunity, and this also accounted for large numbers of deaths.

Today, the Taino no longer exist as a nation. There are remnants of the Taino scattered throughout the Caribbean and Florida who are descendants of the few who hid in the mountains and hills of Kiskeya, or what is now Hispaniola. They have formed a loose confederation of the remaining Taino peoples.

Guacanagari, the cacique who met and helped Columbus, died while hiding in the mountains.

The Timucua, Tekesta, and Calusa, all of Florida, and who were mentioned in the story, met the same fate as the Taino after Ponce de Leon discovered Florida. The remnants of those tribes joined the Seminoles, who were not native to Florida, but were actually breakaway Creeks who fled to Florida from the Creek nation in the Carolinas and Georgia.

The End
~~*~~

About the Author

Donald H Sullivan is a native of St. Augustine, Florida. He started his writing career shortly after retirement from the U.S. Army. He welcomes comments about this book or about any other books he has written. He can be reached by e-mail at dhsully@gmail.com

Other books by Donald H Sullivan:
Turnbull's Slaves
Our Canine Companions Featuring Whiskers
Tales of Wonder
Three Amazing Tales
Tales of Suspense and Mystery
Terrific Tales of Sci-fi and Space Opera
Frankenstein and the Zombies
Chillers
The Magical Earth
The Psionic Man
Marxism and Political Correctness
Whiskers
Vietnam: Reflections of an Interrogator
Taino
A Profile of Dementia
For more information on Sullivan's books, check his website:
dhsully.wix.com/part1

Printed in Australia
Ingram Content Group Australia Pty Ltd
AUHW021823121223
387852AU00007B/100

9 781105 539978